P9-CCM-049

The Enchanted World

SEEKERS AND SAVIORS

The Enchanted World
SEEKERS AND SAVIORS

by the Editors of Time-Life Books

The Content

Time-Life Books · Alexandria, Virginia

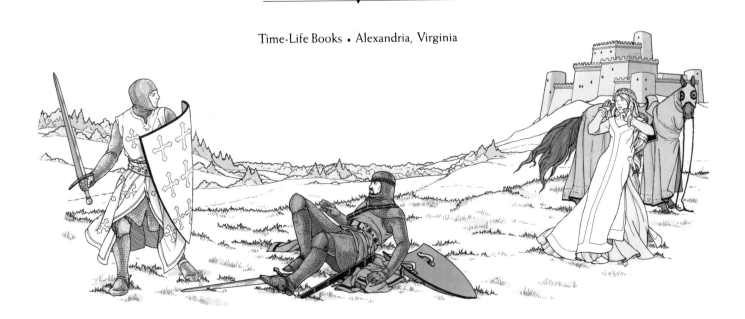

the game. When it was safely spitted and roasting over the fire, filling the little room with its scent, he took a pull from the wine bottle. Then he said to the now-dozing cat, "Is your work hunting?"

Without opening its eyes, the cat said in a sleepy voice, "Better than that, Master, although I like a little sport. I have indeed hunted today, and my catch was greater than what you see. I offered a brace of pheasant to your seigneur as a gift from the Marquis de Carabas. The wine comes from your lord."

"Who is the Marquis de Carabas?"

"You, master. I took the liberty of improving on your condition. No one knows his neighbor in these benighted valleys."

The miller's son whistled. Then he asked with some curiosity, for he had never ventured into the seigneur's fortress, "What is my lord's palace like?"

"What you would expect: damp stones, the wind whining through the windows, pigs rooting among the rushes in the hall and a great pile of manure by the gate. The seigneur was most interested in my master, the rich Marquis. He has a very pretty daughter—no, thank you, I prefer my meat uncooked." The miller's son chewed thoughtfully on a pigeon wing while he considered the matter. The fire crackled; the wind sighed outside; the cat, its paws tucked snugly under its body, purred. When its master spoke again, it flicked an ear at him. "You propose that I marry the daughter of the seigneur and bring her to this place? A fine homecoming that would be."

"I propose that you marry the seigneur's daughter. You are my master because your father named me among his possessions, but I like to live in a well-run household with a mistress to make it comfortable. Not here, and not in your lord's drafty fortress. There are other valleys besides this poor one." The miller's son had to be content with that. The cat sank into sleep beside the fire and said no more.

T he next days passed in the same way as the first. The cat hunted by day; at night it brought game to eat, increasingly detailed descriptions of the seigneur's daughter and the seigneur's interest in marrying her well. After some weeks had gone by, it announced that it had found a home for the Mar-

"Save my master!" cried the cloaked and booted cat, and through enchantment, it convinced
a nobleman that a miller's son was a lord himself, fit to marry the nobleman's daughter.

quis de Carabas to take her to. The time had come for action, said the cat.

Accordingly, the following morning, the miller's son set off into the forest with his cat. The young man carried the beast's cloak and boots because the cat, now trotting by his side, tail erect, eyes bright with interest, preferred to remain unencumbered until it needed the disguise of a man. From time to time, it darted into the underbrush, attracted by sounds or smells the miller's son did not notice.

At a place in the wood where the trees thinned and a mountain river poured down beside the road that led from the castle, however, the cat's behavior changed. It pounced upon its boots and cape and once again grew and wavered in the young man's sight, so that now it seemed a man and now a cat in costume. Then it turned on its master.

"Strip," it hissed, "and walk into the river." Such was the force in its golden eyes and the threat of its curving claws that the young man obeyed. Peeling off his clothes, he stepped into the icy current. Claws gripped his head and pushed him under. He struggled, lungs bursting; blackness pressed upon his eyes.

ow long he struggled before release came, he could not tell; it seemed an eternity before his head broke the surface. He flailed, gasping. Strong hands gripped his wrists and pulled him up onto the bank. His rescuer was a heavy, white-haired man of middle age, clothed in threadbare velvet.

"My lord," said the miller's son, shivering in his nakedness. But he was forestalled. Behind the seigneur was the cat-man, wringing his hands and crying a steady stream of lamentation.

"Brigands, lord. Brigands took my master the Marquis's clothes and gold and tried to drown him. Oh, cover him if you can, quick, before he dies of the cold."

The seigneur wrapped the miller's son in his own cloak and led him through the wood to the road, where his own carriage had halted. It was a shabby, tattered carriage, old-fashioned in make, drawn by a pair of nags that would have best been at the knacker's. But the young man, who had never ridden in a carriage, thought it very fine. And the woman who sat in it, peering anxiously at him, was as pretty as a morning in May, although the gown she wore was of plain gray stuff and the shoes on her little feet were patched. The miller's son huddled in his borrowed cloak, and had the sense to hold his tongue.

He had little need for speech. His cat-servant talked steadily and smoothly, urging him into the carriage with the maiden and her father, describing the way to the Marquis's home, always talking. They clattered through the valley, where bare trees nodded and brown leaves blew, up into mountain mists and past miles of shadowed forest. Finally they descended through thinning woods into sunlight.

A different landscape lay spread out before them. Broad fields of grain, golden with a late, rich harvest, stretched across the valley floor, broken by orchards; the far hillsides were terraced with vines. In the fields and orchards, countryfolk worked, and even from the road the travelers could hear the sound of their laughter.

"Fair country," said the seigneur, and his daughter nodded and smiled.

"The demesne of my master of Carabas," the cat-man said, and its voice, thought the miller's son, was like a purr. He glanced at his companions, but they apparently had noticed nothing. Perhaps they saw the booted cat always as a man, and not sometimes as a cat and sometimes a man. Even when it fixed its golden eyes on a reaper standing near the road and hissed, they seemed to notice nothing. As for the reaper, he pulled his forelock and saluted the miller's son as his lord.

Along the road they bowled, down a grand avenue of oak to a handsome manor house whose servants came running into the courtyard to greet them. Chattering about proper clothing and hissing orders, the cat-man led the miller's son into the house and through its corridors to a quiet chamber; nimble as the best of valets, he dressed the youth.

"What is this?" asked the young man when they were alone.

"A sorcerer's house. Never fear, it is your house now," replied the cat, holding up an embroidered waistcoat.

"And where is the sorcerer?"

"Dead, through a little trick of mine. I asked him to show me how he could shift his shape. He turned himself into a mouse, and I ate him. His people were eager for a new master."

How much of this was true, the young man could not say. He spent the rest of his life in that pleasant house, with the sei-gneur's daughter as his wife. She kept him well-fed and contented. His cloaked and booted servant vanished shortly after he was safely married. At his orders, however, the brown-and-white cat that lounged in sunny windows, slept on every hearthrug and – from time to time – tormented the dovecote, was given all the comforts and indulgences a prince of cats could desire.

The story of the brindled cat did not say how the beast acquired speech or how it could act in the role of a man. The tellers of the tale never thought to question the matter, because they lived in a world where humankind had only lately arrived, a world still shot through with incomprehensible forces and old enchantments.

These rough magics manifested themselves in a bewildering variety of ways – in such intelligent animals as the miller's cat, in beings who had human form but were not human, in unseen powers that could change the shapes of things or even open the door between death and life. Their nature was unknown: The life of the elder world followed no rules that men and women could understand. Sometimes these powers were inimical to mortals, because humankind had intruded on the earth that once was theirs. When that happened, people had to defend one another together or courageously stand alone, using the human virtues of loyalty and love as defenses against inhuman enemies. But when, by some unfathomable caprice, the beings and the powers of the elder age of the world inclined favorably toward humanity, then men and women could control them, and use them as weapons in mortal affairs.

From the tales of that time, it would seem that those humans best able to summon enchantment to their aid were women. An aura of power veiled them, no matter how poor and weak they might be, and this is not surprising: Within their bodies they contained the mystery of life. Indeed, the early generations of humankind worshipped the mother goddess above all – she who was the earth and created from herself whatever lived on or in it, who gave life to the living and received the dead into her soil. She had a thousand names and a thousand faces: Innanna in Sumeria, Ishtar in Babylon, Isis in Egypt, Cybele in Rome, Demeter in Greece, Gertha in Scandinavia. Isis sang, "I am she that is the natural mother of all things, mistress and governess of the elements, chief of the powers divine, queen of all that are in hell, the principal of them that dwell in heaven, manifested alone and under one form of all the gods and goddesses." And even in later centuries, when Isis and her kind had faded from memory and been replaced by younger, different gods, a portion of the mother goddess's mystery clung to all women.

It was partly for this reason, some folk said, that the officers of the new religions preached against women. Jewish men's prayers, for instance, included thanks that they were not women. And the early fathers of the Christian church were virulent in their abuse. They debated whether women had souls, and there was universal agreement that women were instruments of the devil, to be feared and shunned by those who sought true holiness.

The common folk echoed these fears. They believed that women had special access to enchantment. They thought – rightly – that women were especially fierce in the protection of their young, the human race's future. In aid of their offspring, the storytellers said, women called on the invisible powers of the world.

The more ferocious of mothers used sorcery. Icelanders, for instance, told the tale of a widow named Katla, mistress of a prosperous farm at Mávahlid on the west coast of the island, and mother of a son named Odd, whom she dearly loved and whom she guarded with magic. She made her son a cloak that protected him against the bite of steel so that he was not injured in the feuds common in that harsh age. And on one occasion, Katla put her life at risk to shelter Odd with *sjónhverfing* – or "sight blinding." It happened this way:

Odd, a malicious and violent young man, won himself the enmity of his mother's rival in power, a woman named Geirrid, whose lands at Holt marched along the borders of Mávahlid. He accused Geirrid of hagriding – that is, of enchanting one of her neighbors and then using him for a steed at night, when she went about her witch's business.

Geirrid was acquitted of the charge in court, and no more might have come of the matter except bad feeling. Then, however, Odd turned his venomous tongue against Geirrid's son Thórarin, bringing humiliation on him because of something that happened in a battle between Thórarin and his neighbors. That battle was interrupted by the wives of the fighters, who

13

As a suitable home for his master's bride, the cat provided a fine manor house, servants
and rich lands—all stolen from a sorcerer less wise in magic than the smooth-spoken feline.

threw their cloaks over the sword blades. Their action stopped the fight, but at a cost: In the struggle, the hand of Thórarin's wife was severed. Odd, who was present, said Thórarin had done it himself, and this, by the curious humor of the age, made Thórarin a laughingstock. But his mother Geirrid did not laugh. She brooded for a few days, staring into her fire, and then she sent her son and his companions in search of Odd and vengeance.

Twelve young men, red-haired, red-faced, swinging unsheathed swords, strode across the snow-covered fields to Katla's farm. They stamped across the stableyard, shoved open the high, carved door of the house and strode into Katla's chamber, bringing the winter with them.

But the chamber held only women. On the transdais—the long, wooden bench that ran along the gable end of the chamber—sat the mistress of the house, shadowy in the light from the chamber's central hearth. Her only movement was the rhythmic rising and falling of her arm: She was spinning flax, using a distaff to draw the fibers out. In a corner, two of her women worked at a standing loom, whispering to each other. No one else was in sight.

"We have come for your son Odd," said Thórarin loudly.

"Lower your voices and put away your swords," snapped Katla. "Odd is hunting. There is no man here, as you see."

"Then we will search," said Thórarin.

Katla shrugged and went on spinning.

The search was in vain; Odd was not to be found. Frustrated, the young men clattered out of the house, slamming the great door behind them.

Within an hour they returned, disturbed by the memory of Katla's preternatural calm and steady spinning. She had left off spinning and now stood as if on guard in the dim entrance of the house, grooming a buck goat. Behind her in the hall, the distaff lay on the transdais.

"She is sight blinding us," muttered one of the men. "Odd is hidden in the distaff." He strode across the hall and broke the gleaming rod in two.

If Odd had indeed been transformed, he would have resumed his true shape when the distaff broke—but nothing happened. Katla looked up from the animal she held and gave them a sour smile. "Brave men, to break a woman's distaff," she said. They pushed past her and left the place again.

Yet once more they returned, convinced, after they thought the matter over, that they had been tricked by women's magic. This time they saw nothing except Katla, standing by the hearth fire in the hall. They hardly noticed the boar that lay on a pile of ashes in the yard, and again they left without the man they sought. By now, their tempers had cooled. Led by Thórarin, they trudged to his mother's house and told her what had happened.

With narrowed eyes, Geirrid took a sealskin sack from her bride chest. She flung a blue cloak across her shoulders and shepherded her son and his men to the house of her enemy Katla.

They found Katla seated on the transdais, white as death. She ignored the men who gathered around her. To Geirrid she

Spirits of the well

Spirits surviving from the first age of earth sometimes showed themselves to mortals in strange forms indeed. One such appearance occurred during the days when Britain was a land of many kingdoms. The witness was the King of Colchester's daughter, and her adventure began with banishment.

Jealous of the maiden's beauty, the stepmother of the Princess sent her into exile with no more than a loaf of brown bread, a wedge of hard cheese and a pot of small beer tied up in a rough linen bag. The Princess made her way through wood and valley until she came to a place closed in with thorn hedges and pock-marked with caves. In the mouth of one cave crouched a small man, gray as the rock and crooked as the thorn branches. He gazed at the Princess with bright eyes and asked why she walked alone. To seek her fortune, she said bravely. And what had she in the bag? For answer, she offered him food and drink. And when he had feasted, he smiled on her and gave her certain directions.

Following them, the Princess made her way through a hedge of thorn to a clearing where a stone well stood. She sat down beside it. At once, a round object bobbed up in the water. It was a head with golden hair.

"Wash me, comb me, lay me down softly," it sang in a high, whistling voice. The Princess did as she had been bidden – for that head and for two more that appeared after it. And when she was done, the bodiless creatures chattered softly to one another.

"What shall we give her?" one said.

"Beauty to charm the greatest of princes; body and breath scented with flowers; a king to find and love her."

And that is what happened: She continued on her journey; in the next valley a King found and loved her. He sheltered her as his own all his life.

The old man and the heads were later found by other humans, it was said. But rewards were only for the kindhearted. People who displeased the heads were given leprosy and foul stink instead of beauty and perfume.

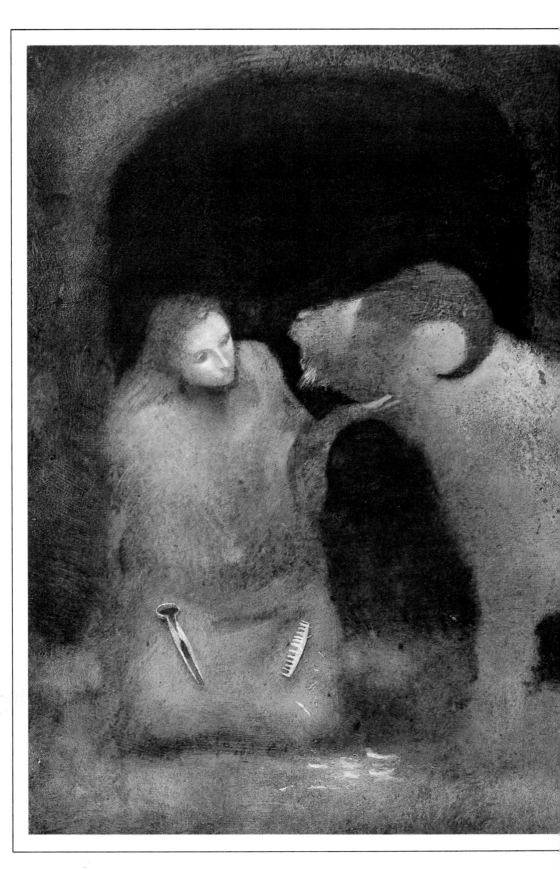

Among mortals, women were best able to call upon the enchantment that flowed in the
world, using the power of spells to shield their children. Thus, Katla the Icelander hid her
son from his enemies by changing his shape to a distaff, then a goat and then a boar.

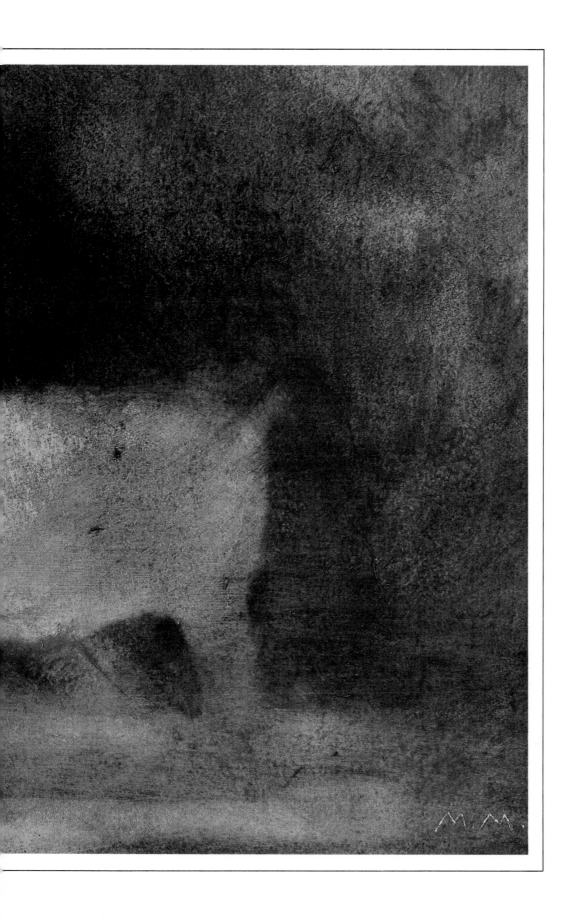

said, "I knew there could be no more sight blinding when I saw your blue cloak. Spare my son, mother of sons."

But Geirrid threw the sack over Katla's head to keep her from casting the evil eye. Thus she banked the fires of sorcery.

"It is you who are the hagrider," said Geirrid. The hooded head bowed assent.

"It was Odd who cut off the hand of Thórarin's wife." Again the nod.

"This distaff was Odd. The goat was Odd, the boar was Odd and this was your doing." Katla bowed her head a third time.

So the men knocked Katla aside and dragged Odd from beneath the long bench where he was hidden: In the face of her rival's power, Katla had not been able to give him another shape. Knowing that spells protected him from steel, the men decided to kill Odd by hanging. They dragged the mother into the stableyard to watch the death of her son. Then, while the body still jerked and twitched on the rope, they picked up stones and made a circle around her: Death by stoning was the punishment for witchcraft. She screeched that she cared little about death, now that her son had been taken from her. Geirrid cast the first stone. It shattered Katla's skull and silenced her forever.

This was an ugly tale, reflective of a cruel age. Even when times grew gentler, men and women sang of mother love as fiery as Katla's. For instance, the Danes said that, in defense of her children, a woman could transcend death, and Danish tales of maternal ghosts were common. Some of these tales were mere frag-

ments, glimpses of events long forgotten. Danish ballads, for example, told of young Svejdal, a lordling cast under an enchantment that denied him rest until he found and wed a fairy woman who had seen and desired him. Despairing – for all he knew of the woman was that she lived across the sea – he wept at his mother's grave. His tears brought her up from the soil, armed with enchantment. Before she sank to rest again, his mother's shade provided the son with a horse that could take him through the most dangerous of forests and across the most treacherous of seas, and she made him invincible by providing a sword dipped in dragon's blood. Svejdal then crossed unknown lands and waters until at length he rested safe in the arms of the woman he sought.

Some of the tales of the dead give more vivid pictures of maternal ghosts. Such a one was Sölverlad, a young woman so fair she was called a "lily wand" by the storytellers. For more than eight years, she was the wife of a knight named Bjorn. She bore him seven children as fair as herself, and she cherished these children tenderly. The house was rich with servants, but Sölverlad fed her young ones herself and wove on her own loom the blankets that warmed them through the Danish nights.

But Sölverlad died young, swept away by plague, and her children – one still in the cradle – were left in the servants' charge until Bjorn brought home a second wife. This woman was hostile to the brood, since their claims on Bjorn came before those of any children she might bear. It was said that when she first entered her husband's hall, magnificent in her scarlet cloak, the smallest of Sölverlad's children clustered at her feet and called her "Mother"; she pushed them away with her booted heel. This may have been mere storyteller's invention. In any case, the new wife, whose name was Blidelil, banished the children to the attic to sleep on straw. As they huddled together to keep warm, their desolate whimperings drifted out across Bjorn's pastures to the tomb where Sölverlad lay. Sölverlad heard, and answered.

On a night not long after the marriage, Sölverlad's eldest daughter, awake and watchful while the small ones slept, saw movement at the door of the attic room. An odor of damp earth and the sickly sweet smell of decay crept into the chamber. Footsteps dragged at the sill; then a lean and tattered creature slid through the door. It had the golden hair of the girl's mother, but its face was no more than parchmenty skin stretched on a framework of bone, and its eyes were dark and empty. While the daughter watched, frozen in place, this creature moved slowly from pallet to pallet, plucking at the straw and caressing the sleeping children's hair, and as it walked, it wept. Then it left the room.

The end of the tale was told by Bjorn himself. He was roused from sleep by a fist hammering on his chamber door. The door slammed open, and there stood the white figure of Sölverlad, clods of earth matting her hair. A bony finger wavered in the air.

"Keep my children safe and warm, Bjorn," said Sölverlad. "If I must come to you again, the watchhounds will howl around this house all night. And after that, Blidelil will suffer so that she will beg for death before she dies." Then the figure dragged itself out of sight. Shaken, Bjorn awakened his new wife and told her what he had seen. And Blidelil acknowledged the power of the ghost. For the rest of her life, she masked whatever feelings she might have harbored, and kept Sölverlad's children according to their mother's wish.

Children deprived of their mothers were guarded in other ways. According to the old tales, they were often defended by animals—wild animals such as wolves or deer or birds or serpents, or domestic ones such as calves or lambs. Sometimes the animals were thought to be inhabited by the spirits of the mothers; sometimes they seemed to serve the mothers' shades; and sometimes they evidently acted for reasons of their own, as did the cat that came to the aid of the French miller's son.

From the vantage of a more prosaic age, it is hard to imagine a world teeming with secret life that might at any moment intrude upon the affairs of humankind. In those days, everything in nature was charged with intelligence. Trees were not mere rooted sleepers, for instance; they were alive with awareness and feeling. Although they mostly remained aloof from the activities of toiling humankind, it was said in Britain that certain oak forests could be moved to action by human suffering. Victims of pursuit would find sanctuary in those woods: Great branches, creaking and groaning, would bend behind them, to snatch and strangle whoever sought to violate the refuge.

Birds—aerial spies that watched with

The fisherman's benefactor

Who knew where magic power might reside? A poor fisherman of Cornwall found it in a flounder that he caught. When he pulled the fish from the water, it spoke in his own tongue, and because it had human speech, the fisherman let it go. In return, the flounder offered prosperity – and he might have kept it, but for his termagant of a wife.

When she heard the tale, the woman looked at the hovel in which she and her husband lived and demanded a proper cottage. Reluctantly, the fisherman returned to the shore and called for the flounder. It surfaced, staring at him with its flat eyes.

"My wife begs a boon," said the fisherman.

"What is it?"

"A proper cottage."

"Go home, then. She has it."

And so she did, a tidy cottage set in a garden. But she was satisfied for only a few days. Then she sent the fisherman back to the sea with new demands. She wanted a castle; she wanted to rule the land as a queen and live in a larger palace; she wanted an empire. Each time, the flounder gave what she asked. Each time the fisherman approached the sea, however, the waves were darker and rougher.

On a day of wind and storm, the fisherman trudged to the shore for the last time. The flounder was waiting, tossing in the swells.

"What does she want now?" it said.

"She wants to be God."

Thunder cracked; the water crashed. The flounder's eyes glimmered in the gloom, and it said, "Too much asked. Nothing will be given. She goes back to the hovel, as before." So the fisherman returned to poverty, hard days of harvesting the sea, and dreary nights of scolding by his thwarted wife.

sharp eyes the doings of the beings on the ground – sang in hidden harmonies full of wisdom and prophecy, and a lucky few mortals acquired understanding of the avian commentary. Understandably, scholars devoted considerable attention to the means of gaining such skill. Some quoted the Roman naturalist Pliny, who wrote that the eating of white snakes conferred comprehension of the birds. Others thought a hawk's tongue placed under their own would provide the gift. Some said it came from drinking dragon's blood.

Even the most domestic of animals had links to a life usually veiled from human eyes. All the year long, cows and sheep grazed placidly in pastures, goats browsed among hedgerows, and chickens pecked busily in farmyards. But countryfolk said that on Christmas Day, from midnight to dawn, the animals were permitted to speak freely: All that night, from cowshed and sheep byre, stable and henhouse, came the rippling whisper of their talk.

Suspicion of the furred and feathered strangers who served humankind was not stilled by the tale of the cat that spent year after year at the farmhouse fire, making no more sound than a mew or a purr until its master arrived to tell the household that the neighboring barn cat had been killed. "Is it so?" said the hearth cat, pricking up its ears. "Then I am the King of the Cats." And it shot out of the house to take its place in a hidden community whose existence humans sensed but never could define.

People rarely had more than glimpses of the secret lives of domestic animals and rarely received anything more than fleeting aid. But in at least one case, an animal servant provided guardianship so devoted as to survive even death. That occurred in Germany, in a time when the country was a patchwork of kingdoms and principalities, some large and grand, some small, some prosperous and some not. In one of these places – little more than a sizable estate – a woman ruled, but her lands were poor, and she fell mortally ill before she had time to repair the kingdom's fortunes. Still, she had the consolation of knowing that her daughter's future was secure: She had betrothed the child at birth to the son of a princely cousin. Now the maiden must travel to the Prince's distant court to meet and marry the young man.

Therefore, the Queen dispatched messengers to her cousin, and some days later, she sent her daughter on her way, providing her with what she could: The horse the maiden rode was the Queen's own steed; its saddlebags held the Queen's own jewels; and her escort was the Queen's lady-in-waiting, a young woman of good but impoverished birth who had spent her life as an object of royal charity. To protect her daughter, the Queen gave her a talisman – a square of cambric stained with three drops of the Queen's blood. Such objects had strong powers in those days.

The two young women set off on a day in August, when the sun beat on the fields and the air was so still that the buzzing of the bees in the wild flowers was loud in their ears. Soon the horses' coats gleamed with sweat, and they slowed to a walk.

The Princess was a timid soul and said

When they spoke of motherhood's magic powers, Danes told of a
       woman who rose from the grave because her children were mistreated. In this
way, she frightened her husband into giving the young ones proper care.

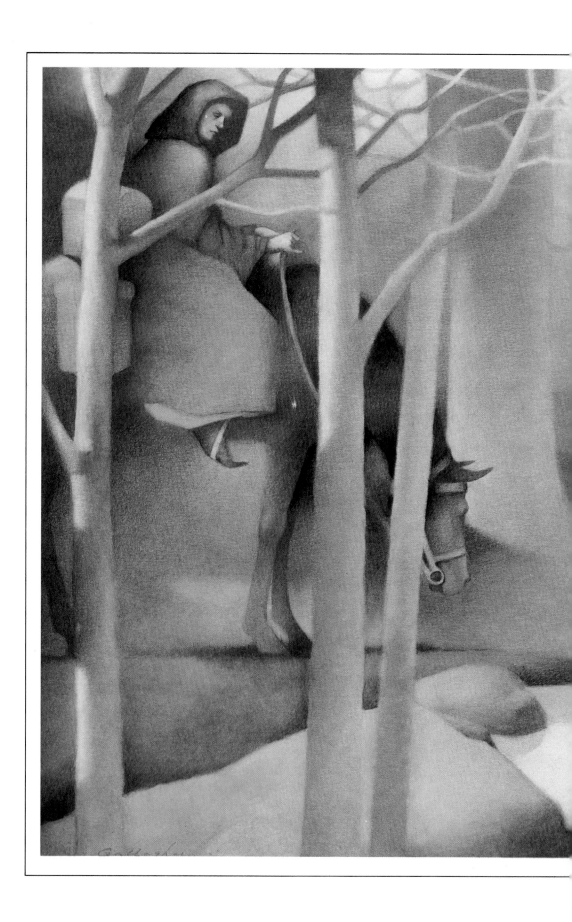

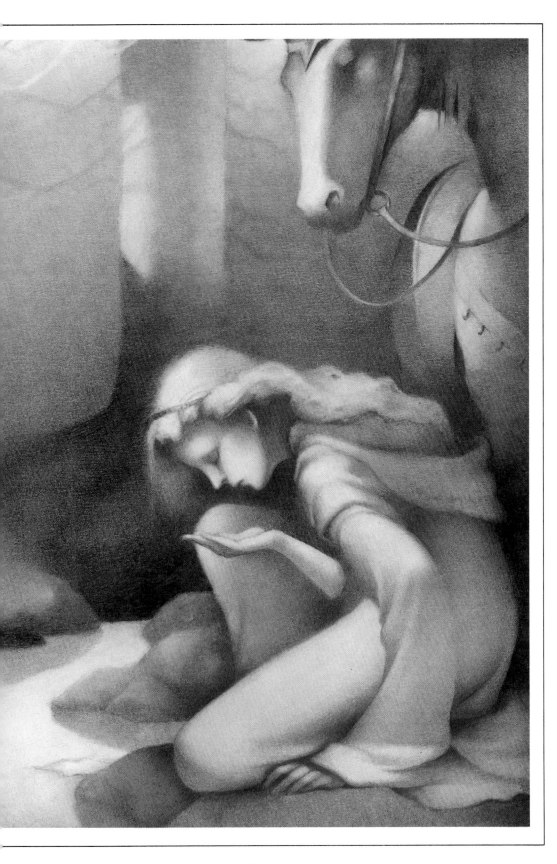

In Germany once, a Queen's daughter journeying to her wedding lost her mother's protective talisman in a stream. Her envious lady-in-waiting, watchful for just such an opportunity, took the Princess's place and forced her into servitude.

little. She was preoccupied with the loss of home and with fears of the cousin she had never seen. Besides, her mother's lady-in-waiting was a sharp-tongued creature, given to public propriety and private gibes. Tired and increasingly hot, the Princess drooped in her saddle and kept her thoughts to herself.

When the path turned into a cool little wood where a stream ran, however, she brightened. She turned in the saddle to the woman who rode behind her and said in her light voice, "Dismount, if you please, and bring me water from the stream."

It was not an unusual request. The waiting woman had served the Queen that way on many a hunt. But the response was a surprise.

"Get it yourself," said the Princess's companion.

The Princess gazed at her, baffled. But the eyes that met her own were level and mocking. The waiting woman's mouth twisted in a tight smile. So the Princess dismounted, sliding to the ground without a block or a hand to steady her, and knelt by the stream to drink. She did not even notice that the square of cambric she had tucked in her bodice slipped out as she bent and vanished in the current of the brook. But her companion saw the talisman go. When the Princess stood up, the waiting woman was beside her. She caught the maiden's arm in a cruel grip.

"Now, then, my girl," she said. "You will be a poor relation and bring me water when I ask for it." The Princess pulled back, then winced with pain as the grip on her arm tightened: She was no match for the other woman.

Within a quarter of an hour, the two had changed clothes and condition. The waiting woman mounted her Queen's fine horse; the Princess scrambled onto the waiting woman's nag. The waiting woman made a final demand: "Swear on your mother's honor that you will tell no living soul of this."

The Princess shook her head.

"If you do not swear, I will kill you now," said the woman. Her eyes glittered. The Princess swore the oath.

When the words were said, the waiting woman kicked her horse. But the horse would not move. The waiting woman glanced back, and the Princess said helplessly, "Forward, Falada, at my command."

"Alas, Queen's daughter," said the horse. "If thy mother knew, it would break her heart." Nevertheless, the horse stepped forward onto the path.

The dismal journey lasted many days. Finally the two young women arrived at the court of the Princess's cousin. It was a charming hill palace, lifting a jumble of towers above a red-roofed village whose streets were garlanded in flowers to greet the Princess. Her mother's messenger had arrived, it seemed—and gone away again. No familiar face greeted her.

The King of the little country waited by the palace gate with his son, and the son helped the waiting woman down from Falada's saddle. He smiled at the Princess, seated quietly on her nag, but the waiting woman forestalled him, saying "We must find her some employment, lord. She was

Reduced to the role of goosegirl, the Queen's daughter was tormented by
a servant while she tended the flocks. But a magical guardian would deliver her.

a good companion, but she is not used to houses." Then she entered the castle on the Prince's arm.

That was the last the Princess saw of her tormentor for many weeks. Servants came and took her horse; they gave her a pallet in a shed behind the castle kitchens, and they sent her every day into the mountain pastures to shepherd geese with the castle gooseboy.

It was not a bad life for one shackled by her own oath. The geese were silly and dirty, but very little trouble. The boy who tended them, however, was insolent. He sneered at her clothes, poorer than his own; he tried to clasp her soft hands, and he plucked at the golden hair that fell about her shoulders.

The last was intolerable; when it happened she gave an angry, miserable sob and cried out, "Blow, winds, and sweep this boy's hat away."

And the winds, by some miracle, blew. The straw hat that the boy wore lifted and danced away across the pasture. He raced off after it, and while he ran and climbed,

The guardian of the Princess-goosegirl was an enchanted horse.
Its fidelity was such that even after death, when its head was nailed
to a city gate, it spoke to give her comfort and reveal her rank.

the Princess braided and pinned up her hair so tightly that he could not pull at it.

This unpleasant little scene was repeated the next day and the next, but worse was to come than the boy's torment. One evening as the Princess walked into the town behind the waddling, hissing geese, she saw nailed to the arch of the town gate the head of her mother's horse. The animal was freshly killed: Blood was just drying on the stones, and the horse's brown eyes were open, gazing into her own.

The boy beside her was a gossip, always underfoot in the kitchens, always ready with the talk of the servants. "The new Princess had it done, because the horse angered her. She is a stern lady," he said.

The Princess herself wept as if for the death of childhood and hope.

"Alas, Falada," she said to the head that hung above her.

The velvet eyes gleamed; the mouth moved. "Alas, Queen's daughter," said its familiar voice. "If thy mother knew, her heart would break."

The gooseboy stared. Then he gave a little crow of fear and scampered off to the kitchens to tell his tale.

The next night, the Princess spoke to the horse's head again, and again it replied with sorrow and admonition. But when its voice faded and she bent her head again to the flock before her, a man stepped out of the evening shadows by the gate. It was the King. He regarded the Princess thoughtfully for a moment and then said, "You are not a goosegirl, maiden. I wondered when first I saw you, and this magic tells me so. Give me the truth, and not the servants' gossip I have heard today."

The Princess shook her head. "I am bound to silence by my own oath, lord."

"Lady, I cannot help if you will not act in your own behalf. Courage: Is there no living thing you can tell of your plight?"

There was no living thing. The oath had been explicit.

"Then tell something that does not live," said the King. His words were short, but his voice was kind. He left her, and she herded the geese into the kitchenyard.

A day went by. The boy teased her. On the arch, Falada lamented as before. The horse's voice was softer now; its hold on life was fading. Soon she would be entirely alone. And that night, when the kitchen fires were banked to glowing coals and the scullery maids snored on their pallets, the Princess knelt at the hearth and, in the softest of whispers, told her tale to the fire. After she had done so, a man rose up from the darkness of the hearth corner. It was the King.

That was the end of the deception. It was said that before he revealed the truth, the King asked the false Princess how she would punish a servant who betrayed her.

"Put her naked into a nail-studded barrel and drag her through the streets," was the woman's reply. And that, according to the storytellers, was the woman's own fate.

As for the true Princess, she regained her place, and the Prince became her husband, as had been promised when the two were in their cradles. The horse Falada, the faithful, the tenacious, never spoke again. The enchantment that gave it voice lasted only until its duty was done.   🦢

An Undying Guardianship

This is the tale of a Scottish maiden whose life was guarded by the spirit of her own dead mother. The girl was quite small when her mother died, and her father brought a new wife home to his manor soon enough. This woman was a widow, with daughters of her own to provide for, and she looked with unkind eyes on the pale child her predecessor had left behind. Then the father himself died, and the little girl, frightened by the cold stranger who had her in charge, retreated to the servants' hall, with its familiar faces. One by one, however, those faces disappeared, to be replaced by other servants, harsh people with little time to spare for the girl. They called her Rashin Coatie – or "coat of rushes" – because, lacking a mantle to keep out the cold, she wore a coat of plaited rushes, as if she were the child of the poorest of crofters.

Years passed. Rashin Coatie grew, and she took to wandering in the Border-country hills. Whenever she ventured out, a companion joined her – a black lamb that frisked at her heels. She crooned lullabies to the little beast

and whispered in its ear, and the servants said
that the lamb answered her in kind.

Word of Rashin Coatie's wanderings caught
the attention of her stepmother, who saw with
disfavor that the pale child had grown into a
golden maiden: However ragged she might be,
Rashin Coatie was an unwelcome contrast to
the woman's own dark daughters. With dour
remarks about idleness, therefore, the woman
issued orders concerning her stepdaughter,
and her servants obeyed, knowing whom they
had to please. Rashin Coatie became a servant
herself, set to work to earn her keep.

She spent her days in the scullery, clean-
ing after her fellow servants. With chil-
blained hands she scrubbed the henhouse
and bent her head humbly under the henwife's strictures, for there was no one to take
Rashin Coatie's part. She ventured above-
stairs only to sweep and scour the hearths. If
her stepmother and stepsisters observed the
slavey toiling on the flagstones, they did
not acknowledge her. The women gathered their furred velvets out of harm's way
and went about their frivolous business
as if she were not there. Who would
notice the work of
the meanest of
servants? The

stepmother, however, watched Rashin Coatie vigilantly. The woman did not fail to note the glossy sheen of the maiden's hair or the petal-like translucency of her skin or the pretty curves of her body. This was no starveling, fed on kitchen scraps. She took to following the maiden on her round of work, and she rode out on the manor lands at dusk, when Rashin Coatie walked alone, save for the night black lamb, speaking words in its high, bleating voice. Thus, the stepmother saw how Rashin Coatie paused beneath a stand of alders, saw how the lamb kicked up its heels and how a cloth appeared on the grass, spread with a little feast: From the air, a roast fowl shaped itself, with a loaf of white bread and a cup of wine.

The woman's response was swift. In the morning, she had the lamb killed and its carcass left on the cutting table in the scullery. And then the stepmother lingered near, long enough to watch the weeping maiden cradle the beast in her arms; long enough to see her carrying it toward the hills; but not long enough to hear the still-living voice that bade Rashin Coatie bury the body and ask at the graveside for what she needed.

In fact, having disposed of whatever fairy or demon nourished Rashin Coatie, the stepmother paid her little attention. The wom-

an had other things to occupy her mind: The year was drawing in. At the great house of the chief of her clan, Christmas revels were beginning. Her own two daughters would go there, to feast and dance with the chevaliers who attended the great lord, and the result might be well-made marriages and lands far broader than this small manor. With the eyes of inexorable ambition, the woman assessed her daughters; with hands of steel, she laced their gowns tight and bound gems in their hair; with cruel fingers, she pinched their cheeks and lips to redden the flesh.

And it seemed that her efforts were not in vain. In the lord's hall, where mighty oak logs blazed to keep away the cold, where musicians in motley led the galliards and pavans, the daughters sparkled. The eyes of a King's son rested on the younger; the mother saw it and smiled.

But she smiled in vain, for a woman appeared in the hall, a sunlike woman wreathed in summer flowers and gowned in white and gold. In her presence, stillness fell. The dancers faded into shadow. Only the King's son still seemed substantial: He was this woman's mate; any eye could see it. She knelt before him. He raised her to her feet and signaled for the music. Together, clothed in light, they

went down the dance, and as if released from a spell, the revelers joined them.

Hour after hour, the company danced, robes swirling, jewels glittering in the firelight, and always in the midst of the brilliant clouds of color, the starry stranger moved, and the King's son with her. No other woman caught his glance then, and she looked at no other man. Enchantment swathed hall and dancers; they whirled outside time in the formal figures of the dance.

They were not outside time. At the door of the hall a guard called the hour, and high in the fortress, a bell began to toll. It was midnight; a sigh ran through the company and the name of the magic hour seemed to float on the sigh.

With that sigh, the spell was broken. The stranger gasped and halted where she stood, and the dancers drew back a little, confused. Then the woman dropped the King's son's hand, and with a cry, she fled out of the warm hall into the night, the white and gold vanishing into clouds of snow.

The King's son followed, but he returned alone. In his hand was a small golden slipper, fashioned of silk.

"Sir," a knight said, "leave this folly. That was a fairy woman, set free by the season and the hour."

"This is a real slipper, made for a real woman. It is the charm by which I shall find her," the Prince replied. And the stepmother heard and made her plans.

Long weeks passed, interrupted only by rumor. The Prince had ridden north, the gossips said, or he had ridden south. He visited every fortress, every palace, every manor. To every maiden, fair or not, he offered the golden slipper. But the slipper would fit no maiden's foot.

Spring had begun before the Prince arrived at the house where Rashin Coatie lived. The scullery maid was not in evidence. In the manor hall, Rashin Coatie's stepmother waited with her daughters by her side. They trembled; they were reluctant, but they had seen the glitter in their mother's eyes, and they held their tongues.

While the Prince watched, a page proffered the little shoe for the foot of the younger daughter, which was clad in a white stocking stained at the heel and toe with crimson. The shoe fit. Ashen-faced, the maiden swayed in her seat; her mother thrust herself between the young woman and the Prince with a swirl of concealing skirts and sleeves. She hissed a command and stepped back. The maiden arose and curtsied to the Prince.

"A bride for you, lord," said the mother.

The Prince's face was puzzled, but he took the maiden's hand and led her from the hall. He handed her up into the saddle of a palfrey that was waiting, and he mounted his own tall horse. The young woman drooped where she sat, although the cold eyes of her mother were upon her. But then even her mother's attention was diverted.

Over the heads of the riders, a small bird swooped and darted, and as it flew, it caroled a song in words the humans understood. This was the house, sang the bird, but this was not the maiden: The Prince had not yet found his bride. Let him look at the shoe once more.

He dismounted, took his betrothed's shoe in his hand as she sat in the saddle, and felt the hot blood that seeped through the silken slipper onto his hand.

"She cut her own child," sang the bird overhead. The Prince drew off the golden shoe and the stocking, revealing a foot with broken toes and mutilated, bleeding heel.

"Send for the maiden who wears the coat of rushes," called the bird, and it flew up into the branches of a tree, where it preened its wings and watched the humans with round, bright eyes. The Prince turned to the mother. Then, in a voice like the winter wind, he said, "Send for that maiden. And attend to your

daughter's wounds." Without a word, the woman left him, leading her own child, and she did not return.

Some moments later, however, a young woman came into the courtyard, a slight, fair woman, barefoot, clothed in a patched gown. She curtsied to the Prince, but she glanced up toward the tree branches where the bird song floated, and she smiled.

"You are a servant of the house, maiden?" asked the Prince.

"I am the daughter of the house," Rashin Coatie replied.

"And who was your father?"

She told him, and added, "My mother's spirit speaks to me from the body of a lamb buried on the hill and sings for me as that bird sings in yonder tree."

The Prince offered the bloodstained slipper. It slid easily onto the maiden's foot. Again she smiled and the bird song swelled, joined by a chorus from every branch. Light shone around her for a moment; then Rashin Coatie stood revealed in a blaze of gold, clothed in a gown embroidered with gilt.

"You have found me, my lord, and freed me," she said, and she held out her hand.

So by her mother's will, the scullery maid became the Prince's bride. And as for her stepmother, no one knows what became of her.

Chapter Two

Tests of Love and Loyalty

Children of great families dwelled in splendid isolation once: Almost from birth, they lived apart from their parents in their own households, with their own accounts and stewards and hierarchies of servants. This rarefied existence seemed to engender in brothers and sisters a particularly fierce devotion – or so the old tales suggest:

On the west coast of Sweden, seven such children occupied a small palace, a stone building with onion-domed towers, set in a park by a lake and walled around by evergreen forest. There were six boys and a girl – the progeny of a Count of the region. Their mother was dead.

The father saw to it that they were kept in comfort on this estate, the most minor of his holdings, and he had them educated according to their rank. In other ways, however, he paid them little attention. He lived in a greater palace some leagues distant, and he was occupied with the shifting alliances and regional wars of the time.

The children's lives passed peacefully enough – a daily round of tutors and governesses and nurses, of hunting for the boys and even for the daughter, who had her own pony and miniature bow. Her brothers liked to have her with them; in-

deed, the children were very close. When they were together, the palace echoed with their laughter and calls, spoken in the secret patois they used among themselves.

Apart from messengers sent by their father, few outsiders intruded on this enclave. The children were therefore drawn, one spring afternoon, by the sight of a stranger in the park, a woman cloaked in blue and riding a gray horse. The horse cantered easily through the palace gate. By the time the woman had swung to the ground, tossed her reins to a groom and attended to the greetings of the steward, the children had gathered around her. She regarded them for a moment, then said, "Well, children, I am your father's new Countess, come to see how you go on."

She swept into the hall. Entranced, the children followed her through the rooms and up the winding stair that led into the towers of their house. In a high room, she paused, surveying the expanse of flowering park and dark fir forest spread out beneath the windows and the vault of sky above. Then she beckoned to the boys.

They approached quite willingly. She touched each boy's hair. Then she whispered a word, and the boys crowded toward the tower window. Each one leaped

down the stair. She was indeed alone. She wandered through the silent, sunny rooms, calling out from time to time, but no nurse or servant answered. No fires burned in the kitchens, and in the stables no horses stamped. The spell had taken all life from the place, it seemed.

Then Sigurny found a cloak for herself and did as the woman had told her. She walked through the quiet park until she reached a track that led into the forest, where she had often hunted with her brothers. The dark woods closed around her, cool and fragrant and welcoming. Small creatures rustled in the carpet of needles as Sigurny passed; from time to time, a bird sang out. On she walked, through the long spring afternoon, without purpose or hope, while the light faded and the air grew chill.

At dusk, she arrived at a clearing where a wooden house stood — a forester's cottage, perhaps, or a huntsman's retreat. Its door was open, and Sigurny called a greeting. When no answer came, she went inside.

The cottage was a humble one, but cared for. From its rafters hung ceiling dress, the embroidered linen rectangles that countryfolk used. The walls were lined with cupboard beds, each with its carved and painted shutters, its bedstraw

to the sill, and as he leaped, he vanished. In his place, a white swan appeared and launched itself into the air. Soon six of the great birds wheeled outside the walls, white as the clouds that sailed above them. The woman called to them, chanting in an unknown tongue. When her voice ceased, the swans banked, and with powerful wingbeats, headed north.

The Countess watched them go, then turned her gaze to the sister.

"What is your name?" she said.

"Sigurny."

"Ah. I advise you to take to the forest, Sigurny. Your brothers have left you. You will find no protection here." And with a low chuckle, the woman swept past the girl. The Countess's footsteps sounded on the stair; her horse's hoofs clattered on the paving stones below; and then she too was gone. That was the last the girl would see of her stepmother or hear of her father. Her path led away from home.

After a few moments, Sigurny ventured

Cast into swan shape by enchantment, six brothers sailed the skies of
Sweden year after year. But their sister knew the key to the spell: She had to
make them shirts from nettles—and not utter a word until the task was done.

50

and pile of brightly striped feather beds. The floor was strewn with fir twigs. Here was a refuge from the gathering darkness. Sigurny wrapped herself in her cloak, lay down on a bench and fell asleep.

She was awakened by the rushing whistle of swans' wings. In the moonlight that silvered the clearing outside the house were the swans themselves, spiraling to earth. The birds landed, and as their webbed feet touched the ground, their feathers fell away, and Sigurny's brothers stood before her. In a moment she was among them, in their arms.

"Oh, you are free then; we can go home again," she said, and laughed for joy. But they did not laugh in return. They led her into the house and made her sit and told her their fate — how the stepmother had enchanted them, so that only on these spring and summer nights could they take human form again. When winter came, they would fly south to warmer lands.

There is a way to free us," her eldest brother said, "but the Countess set a hard charm on us. If we are to become men, then you must make for each of us a shirt. You must make it from nettles, one shirt each year, for six years, and during that time you may not speak a word or laugh, for if you do, the magic will be shattered and we will remain swans forever."

That was a hard charm indeed. Nettles are bushy, many-flowered herbs whose stalks can provide a coarse fiber. But the process of obtaining the fiber is laborious, and to make it into fabric is even more difficult: The plants' leaves bristle with hairs that leave a painful sting in human flesh. But Sigurny had no one in the world to love except her brothers. She did not hesitate. "I will make the shirts," she said.

And in the next days, she began to work. She gathered the nettles and stripped their stinging leaves with blistered fingers; she pounded the stems to flatten them into fiber. All through that summer she worked. During the long days, her brothers flew as swans overhead or floated in the still waters of the Swedish lakes, gliding over their reflected images with effortless ease. When the last blue light faded each night, they returned to the cottage where their sister toiled, shaking off their bird forms, gathering around her and giving her what comfort they could. She smiled upon them, but she did not break the charm by speaking.

When beech and aspen turned to gold, however, and the wind blew down from the north, the brothers grew restless. Each night they came later to Sigurny's cottage. Each morning they left earlier, until at last, at the dawn of a day when the first frost glittered on the grass, they left her. Sigurny watched them on their way until the last white wing flashed in the sun. She wept, but not a word did she say.

Through that winter she kept close to the cottage. With a wooden distaff, she spun the fiber she had collected into a kind of flax. She ventured out again when the last snows melted and the nettles began to push up through the earth. Then she gathered the stalks again and waited for the beat of swans' wings. But Sigurny's brothers did not reappear, and she spent the summer and the following winter working in solitude and living on what fish she could catch in the forest streams and what plants she could glean from the ground.

Sigurny was only twelve years old when first she entered the forest; she was fourteen when a lone hunter discovered her there. The man was the ruler of one of the small, semibarbarian kingdoms that still survived in the depths of those vast woods. He was rough but kind, and he was charmed by the silent maiden, beautiful despite her blistered hands and ragged dress. When he saw that she was without protection, he said he would take her home with him. She nodded, having no choice, but she gestured toward the cottage, and he waited patiently while she carried out her bags of flax. These he slung behind his saddle; then he set Sigurny on the horse, swung himself up behind her, and headed toward his own lands.

It was a new world that Sigurny entered — a fortress rimmed with palisades, enclosing a square, stone castle and thatched villages of wattle and daub. Life was harsh there, yet touched with a rude splendor. Jewels winked in the sword hilts of the men. The women's robes were fastened with silver and ornamented at shoulder and elbow with spheres of filigree; gilded chains hung across their bosoms.

The women's quarters occupied their own wing of the palace; they were ruled by the only surviving wife of the King's father. She was a bent and sharp-tongued crone who gave scant welcome to the foreign inmate. When she saw the honor the King accorded this silent maiden, the woman held her peace, but she kept Sigurny under her eye. During the day, she watched while Sigurny learned to use the hand loom, and she sneered at the dull flaxen stuff the maiden wove. In the evenings, when the King sent for his prize, the older woman hissed under her breath.

The dowager was silenced when the King married Sigurny. She waited for reproaches from the young woman, but none came. Sigurny never spoke; imperturbable, she continued to weave during the day and to spend her nights with the King. At seasons' change, she watched for the swans that were her brothers. Wedges of the migrating birds sailed over the fortress in the spring and autumn, but none of them descended to her. In the second year of her marriage, she bore a son.

This infant vanished from his cradle two nights after his birth. Sigurny did not speak even then, but the dowager spoke, spewing poison in the King's hall. She said that the King's wife was in league with witches and therefore could not speak with men and women; she said that the wife had murdered the King's child.

Without a sound, Sigurny wept, for she had seen the bent figure hobbling from her chamber, clutching the swaddled bundle that was Sigurny's son. But she said no word, being bound by the charm that she had accepted years before.

"I will not believe it," said the King when he heard of the dowager's accusation, and took his wife's hand. Thus was Sigurny saved from punishment.

Two years later, she bore the King another son, and this child, too, vanished from his cradle. Again the dowager made her accusation of murder; again the Queen was silent. The people of the King's court turned their backs to her, and the King gave the sign that sentenced her to death.

So on a bright morning in the spring of her eighteenth year, Sigurny was led from her chamber to the place of execution outside her husband's castle walls. He waited there with his people. In the center of this place, the headsman stood by his block; his ax was not in sight, being hidden under straw until it was needed, so as not to startle the prisoner.

Sigurny advanced slowly to the block, a slight figure robed in blue, carrying on one arm layers of flaxen shirts. She halted at the place of execution and stood motionless while the waiting women who had walked beside her pinned up her hair from her neck. They offered to take the shirts from her, but Sigurny shook her head, and the women stepped back.

"Wife, will you not speak?" said the King. But she was mute.

The headsman gave a signal. Obeying it, Sigurny knelt before the block. Then the executioner bent to the straw on the ground and withdrew his ax.

At that instant, a high call sounded overhead and was answered by another and another until the air was loud with double descending notes. These were the alarm cries of swans, as the people knew: Although the wild swan most often seen in Europe is named "mute," it can call as well as any bird. Six white shapes plummeted and, rowing the air with great wings, alighted around the figure by the block. The headsman hesitated, confused, and the people muttered among themselves.

The mutters turned to cries of wonder: Sigurny rose and flung her shirts one by one to the birds. The swans' feathers fell away in white drifts to the ground, and six young men stood where the swans had been. The youngest of them had a swan's wing in place of an arm. His shirt had lacked a sleeve.

Sigurny, standing proudly among her brothers, smiled at the King and said, "Now, Husband, I will speak."

She told the King of the charm that had required her silence and had kept her brothers under enchantment; she told of the dowager's deception and of her murder of the King's sons. In the end, it was the dowager's head that fell under the ax. Sigurny was restored to her husband; her brothers were welcomed and honored among his companions. The family made their home there for the rest of their lives.

Such tales of devotion were often told when magic still worked in the world. During the centuries when the human race was young and its power frail in comparison to that of the ancient enchantments that lay hidden everywhere, people clung together. In defending one another, they found the strength that could save them.

The threats to humankind came from many quarters. Sometimes, as in the case

Facing execution, the sister of the swan brothers kept her silence and clutched the shirts that
would make them men again. Then the swans themselves flew to her rescue—and their own.

All the swan brothers were freed from enchantment, but the youngest lived out his life with a wing for one arm. The magic shirt his sister made him lacked one sleeve.

of the stepmother who entrapped Sigurny and her brothers, the enemies were themselves human — men and women who had acquired understanding of the spells that altered human shape or sapped human strength or wove imprisoning nets of illusion. More often, the enemies were alien — members of races far older than humankind. They were beings whose forebears had once ruled the world and who had been driven into hiding by human ambition and strength, by the clearing of forests and the planting of fields, by the building of fortresses and villages and towns. Now these beings — whom humans called fairies or elves or "the old ones" or, euphemistically, "the fair folk" — lay concealed within the earth or under the sea. Some dwelled among humans, but their realms were protected by walls of invisibility. The time of their greatest glory was past, but they had not yet lost all their power, and they did not hesitate to use it against invading humankind. Men and women knew the danger well. They told tales of children spirited away by the fairies, never to be seen again; of mothers wrested from their own infants to nourish the offspring of an elder race with human milk; of maidens and youths enticed into the other world as brides or husbands. Often, people were lost not through de-

sign but through their own carelessness. The veil that curtained the other world sometimes lifted, so that those who did not belong to it might glimpse its mysteries. But such glimpses were full of danger.

The people of Somerset reported that on a hill called Blackdown, not far from Taunton, crowds of little people, gaily clothed in red, blue and green and wearing old-fashioned high-crowned hats, sometimes appeared at night. The gathering reminded observers of country fairs: In the assembly were miniature peddlers and tinkers and booths for selling trinkets, food and ale. The sight was charming and elusive, now appearing, now disappearing; people called it the Fairy Market and realized that a busy world existed just out of reach of their own.

Much attracted by the nocturnal sight, a farmer chose once to ride into its midst. He turned his horse directly to the hill as soon as he saw the lanterns and heard the music, but when he arrived at the place, the fairies had disappeared. He was buffeted and jostled by invisible hands until he retreated, making for home and safety. As soon as he was out of range, he looked over his now-aching shoulders and saw again the lights and the small people. He arrived home lame on one side from the fairies' buffeting, and he remained lame for the rest of his life.

The man was lucky in that he retreated quickly and that he touched nothing belonging to Faerie, as the other world was called. Everyone knew that the mortal who ventured into Faerie might return, but that if he touched fairy gold there, or ate of fairy food, he was lost, for he then fell into the power of the old ones.

This happened to a Cornish farmer, out in the warm air one midsummer night. He came to a field and orchard where a company of shining people danced. Entranced by the music, he drew close, stepping among plum trees where starlight twinkled on every leaf. The plums on the heavy-laden trees seemed to press into his hands; his fingers curled around the warm fruit.

A sharp cry halted him. Out of the glimmering shadows glided the woman he would have married, if she had not disappeared three years before. She warned him against eating the enchanted fruit, for it was the food of the fairies he saw dancing. She had wandered into this pretty place one night and eaten a plum herself, she said sadly. Thus, she had fallen into the fairies' power, condemned to live as their slave forever. So saying, she faded from view. The music became fainter, the dancers disappeared among the trees, and the farmer was left alone in the dark.

Such tales suggested that the beings of Faerie lay in wait for the curious or reckless, seeking an infusion of strong young human blood to increase their strength and allow them to hold back the dark that threatened to envelop their kind. In many times and places, men and women found themselves in a life-or-death fight against the fairy desire to acquire human vigor and thus forestall their doom.

Such a struggle occurred in Scotland once, and it showed how the devotion of humans to one another was their greatest defense. The tale began in the Border country, near the manor house where three brothers and their sister lived. Theirs was a small manor, sturdily built of the local stone, set on a hill, with a village meandering down the slope and the whole surrounded by the long fields and woods that constituted the demesne.

On this particular day, the village basked in summer sunshine. The sister and her brothers idled away the afternoon in a meadow by the squat-towered village church. They were seldom together these days: The young men were in training for knighthood and served the great border lords; the sister stayed at the manor with her mother. So they lounged on the grass and chatted and laughed and teased.

"See the Burd Helen!" cried one of the brothers in broad Scots, referring to her red-gilt hair: "Burd," besides being a title for a nobleman's daughter, meant "fair." From where he lay on the grass, he tossed a leather ball toward the roof of the church and added, "Now find it, there's a good lass." Helen laughed at him and accepted the game. She ran around the church withershins — counterclockwise. As she vanished around the building's corner, the sun shone full in her face, so that her shadow fell behind her. She did not reappear.

After a few moments, the brother shouted her name. He was not answered. He glanced at the others, and all three arose and strode toward the church. They searched around it, laughing and calling. They searched the meadow and the wood beyond, but now they searched silently.

57

"Her shadow fell behind her, where she could not see it," said one brother. The three ceased searching then, and gathered with grave faces to confer.

In those days, people guarded their shadow, knowing that it carried something of its owner's spirit. Many people believed that warriors could kill a man by stabbing his shadow, and this belief was recalled even in later centuries, in the adage that to step on a person's shadow brought the person bad luck. Helen's shadow had been cast where she could not see it mimic her movements. Invisible to its owner, it became vulnerable to any being who chose to trap it. Whoever or whatever had seen Helen's shadow defenseless had taken it — and the maiden with it.

The eldest brother announced, "I shall ride to find her."

"We all will ride," the other two said.

"I, because I am the first-born," the eldest insisted. "If I do not return in a month's time, then follow me."

In a month's time, when he had not returned, the second brother rode out, heading north across the fields into the mountains. He, too, failed to return.

Then the third brother took up the search. This brother was called Childe Rowland — Childe being the title given to young men of important families. Of the three, he was closest in age and heart to Helen; he had spent the two months in an agony of restlessness. At the edge of the manorial lands, he drew his horse to a halt. A stone hut stood there, poised at the brink between the groomed world of humankind and the wilderness of the mountain forests. In the hut lived a reclusive man, said by some to be a scholar, by others a wizard.

Rowland tethered his horse and pushed open the hut's wooden door. The single room was empty, but the man could not be far away. A fire of fragrant apple wood crackled on the hearth. On a polished table lay rolls of vellum — the scholar's books. An owl sat on a window sill, its head tucked under its wing.

"Go away," said a muffled voice. Rowland stared at the window sill. Had the bird spoken?

"That will do," said another voice, and the knight turned swiftly. An old man clothed in rusty cleric's robes and carrying a basket of apples stood beside him. He set the basket on the table, dusted his hands on his robe, and sat down.

"I have been expecting you, young knight," he said at last. "Your brothers have been here before you."

"Where are they now?" Rowland asked.

"Why, they are with your sister, in the tower of Elfland's King," replied the man. He gestured, and Rowland too sat down.

"Sir, how do you know this?"

"A little bird told me," said the scholar with a grin. At the window, the owl roused and settled its neck feathers and rocked on its perch, but it did not open its eyes.

"Tell me how I can find them and bring them home."

"My son," said the scholar, "some things are easy in the saying and hard in the doing. Map," he added, and one of the cylinders of vellum unrolled itself on the table beside him.

Star brothers of the northern sky

To show the transcendent power of fraternal love, the Greeks told the tale of Castor and Pollux, known as the Dioscuri, or "striplings of Zeus." Some said that the god sired these twins on a human woman, so that one was immortal, like the father, and one mortal, like the mother. In any case, they were inseparable in peace or war – Castor being famed as a horseman and Pollux as a boxer.

Castor, the mortal, fell in battle with his brother beside him. In his love and grief, Pollux prayed to his father that he too might die and dwell in the underworld with his twin. But even Zeus could not give death to an immortal. The god therefore translated the brothers into stars, to float forever, singing, in the dome of heaven.

Castor and Pollux still may be seen in the northwestern region of the winter sky, their heads the twinned bright stars of the constellation Gemini. Spartan warriors prayed to them, for they were patrons of the brave; Greek sailors called upon them, for their shining could quiet storms at sea.

"You will go here," said the scholar, tracing a route that led north from the manor lands into the mountains. Beyond the markings that indicated the mountains, nothing showed on the paper.

"Somewhere in these unmarked lands are the dominions of the Elf King. You will know when you have crossed the border, and guides will greet you to lead you to his tower. And when you have reached his lands, here is what you must do: Strike off the head of any person who speaks to you. Any person. Here is what you must not do: Eat or drink anything offered you. The meat and the wine of Elfland have the power to keep you there forever."

Rowland waited, but the old man said no more. The gray head nodded; like his owl, the scholar slept. When Rowland rose to go, however, the sleeper raised his head. "Remember," he said.

So Rowland rode north in easy stages, living on the game he caught and water he took from the wilderness streams, sleeping beneath the trees at night. Beyond the mountains, the land descended to rolling hills, cloaked in the gold of autumn. Past the hills, great rye and barley fields spread out, heavy with grain, but no farmers' villages nestled among them. Rowland rode along a track that led through tall grass, into meadows studded with clusters of trees, before he came upon a living soul.

This was a horse-herd, an old man robed in gray and carrying a long whip. At the appearance of the stranger and his strange horse, the animals came galloping across the pastures with loud whinnies of greeting. They milled around the young knight, and he saw their eyes. Flames flickered there, lights of another world. These were elvish horses. He had crossed into the King's domain.

"Hey, fellow," Rowland cried. "Which is the way to the Elf King's tower?"

"Lord, I cannot tell you, but if you will ride west, you will find a guide," the man replied, squinting up at the stranger.

Rowland nodded. He turned his horse, so that the horse-herd did not see him draw his sword. Then, leaning from the saddle, he swept the blade toward the man's neck. The head fell to the ground; the trunk, spurting blood, swayed for a moment; then it too dropped, and the elvish horses scattered, screaming.

Ignoring them, Rowland sped west. After some hours he came upon a cowman, whose animals had the fiery eyes of Elfland. He questioned this man as he had the horse-herd, and he received the same answer. This man, too, Rowland slew before he rode on.

And at last, on a grassy plain among orchards whose trees drooped with apple and pear, he discovered a round little woman with a staff in her hand and a flock of chickens bustling at her feet. She was a henwife, and she looked harmless enough. Then a bird cocked its head to gaze up at him with one round eye, and he saw the fires leaping in that eye.

"Greetings, mother," said Rowland. "Where is the tower of your King?"

"West, through the trees," she replied. "You will find a hill ringed with three ramparts. Walk withershins once around each one, so that the sun is in your face. On each rampart, call out for the hill to open. It will open, if you are a brave man."

He nodded and turned to go. This was only an old woman after all, and he lacked the heart to murder her. He glanced back. She was regarding him with glittering eyes as round and red as the hens she tended. With a single sword stroke, Rowland killed her. Her head rolled on the ground and vanished among the squawking birds.

Finally, at the end of that autumn afternoon, Rowland found the green hill of the Elf King's tower. Dismounting, he strode its ramparts, facing into the westering sun.

At the crest of the hill, a gate swung open, and Rowland walked through it into shadow. Through vaulted corridors he wandered, hearing only the sound of his boots on the stone and the clinking of his spurs. The corridors descended into the earth; no lanterns guided him, but a faint light shone, enough for him to see his way along the featureless, rocky trail.

It redoubled at last into a lofty hall ringed about with balconies and doors, warm as springtime, glowing like pearl. And here, far from home, he found his sister Helen, fair as she had ever been. She sat on a royal couch draped in silk; when he entered the chamber, her eyes turned toward him, offering the flat, dull stare of the insane or enchanted.

In silence, Rowland advanced. Tears stood in his eyes. He bent and took her icy hands in his own.

"Pity of God that you should come to this place, Brother." Her voice was toneless and very low. ,

But Helen had spoken. He drew his sword. She made no move, and he swung closing his eyes as the blade met flesh.

When he opened them, she stood before him, his own sister, with the light of his own world in her eyes. "Rowland, you have freed me," she said, smiling at him.

"My brothers?"

For answer, Helen gestured toward the shadows, where two coffins lay. "They would not strike the blow that broke the spell," she said. "The Elf King has sent them into a prison of sleep."

Here was a grim case. He had found his sister; he had found his brothers. But they might die in the enemy's hall or in his labyrinth of corridors. The enemy was nowhere to be seen.

"Well, Sister," said Rowland. "We will need our wits about us." Helen nodded, but she could tell him nothing about the plan of the fortress and little about the Elf King. Wrapped in spells, she had passed her imprisonment in a waking dream. The last thing she remembered was running toward the sun and finding her way blocked by a tall man who carried her shadow over his arm as if he held a discarded garment.

Rowland listened to this intently. At length he said, "I thirst. Bring me drink if you can, while I consider." She brought him milk in a golden bowl. The cup was at his lips before his glance caught his sister's look of despair. Still in the Elf King's power, she had to offer Rowland the forbidden drink. With an oath, Rowland hurled the cup of enchantment to the floor.

And as if the ring of the metal on the stone had been a summons, a door flew open and a man surged into the room, a

Once it was dangerous to run toward the sun and leave one's shadow unguarded, for the fairies could take it to their own country. That was how Fair Helen of Scotland became a captive of the King of Elfland.

tall man armored in black who gave a battle cry and raised a sword high over his head. This was the Elf King, come for Rowland's blood. With swiftness born of a lifetime of training, Rowland sprang to meet him.

Thrust and parry, feint and swing, the two knights circled, and all the sound they made was the tearing of their breath and the grunts of effort as they hacked with their swords. The Elf King used no magic now, it seemed: As if his honor required it in combat, he fought the mortal with mortal's weapons. But he was strong and nimble, a canny fighter. His heavy blade glanced off Rowland's shoulder once and then again, and the young knight staggered and fell to

one knee. Up the black blade swung for the death blow, baring the unmailed joint where the King's body armor ended. Rowland struck from underneath. The Elf King screamed. His sword spun from his hands, and Rowland lunged up and forward, bearing his enemy to the floor. He laid his blade across the Elf King's throat. Gasp-

ing, Rowland gathered breath to speak.

But the Elf King forestalled him. "Fairly done, mortal," he said, and his voice was cool and clear. "I yield."

"Free us."

"I will free you."

Rowland rose and stepped back. The dark King also rose. Perfectly composed, he moved around the chamber, touching Helen, touching the two brothers. And when they stood before him, sister and brothers, freed from the dark, he said, "Do not run into the sun again, maiden, if you would remain in your own world. We need your blood in this one, and we are always watching. Now go." He gestured toward the door he had entered. The brothers gathered around Helen and led her to it.

They stepped through the portal into a meadow littered with fallen leaves. At its edge stood the squat tower of their own village church, and on the hill above, the walls of their own manor house. When they looked back, they saw the ghost of an image: the outline of a massive door in the air. It faded, even as they watched.

The brothers and sister had formed a united company; love caused Rowland to pursue his sister and his brothers — and his own intelligence and fighting skill had freed them from enchantment. Such devotion was seen in many families once. And in the ages when humankind formed only a small part of a large and populous world, the same allegiance was seen among people who shared no blood ties at all. Society was shaped then as a network of loyalties: The peasant worked the land and paid fealty to his lord; his lord in turn served a greater lord, and that lord a greater still. In return for their services, the lesser received protection from the greater. Each overlord had the duty to defend his people.

In that warring era, in fact, loyalty was rarely stronger than among warriors who fought side by side against a common enemy. Those who passed through the fire of battle together forged friendships as strong as any brotherhood, and the surviving legends of the great warriors celebrate their passionate devotion as much as their prowess and valor.

Of fighting companies, few displayed such spirit or were bound so closely as the Fianna of Ireland. This army served the island's High King, settling disputes among lesser rulers, defending the people and guarding the harbors against invasion. In the age when they flourished, the Fianna were more than four thousand strong – 150 chiefs, each of whom commanded twenty-seven men. The soldiers were recruited at the aonachs, the great clan gatherings and fairs held several times each year around the country. There, the youths of Ireland proved themselves at seasonal games, maidens were brought to make good marriages, cattle were sold and foreign trade conducted.

Once chosen, the Fianna's recruits were put through a series of tests to prove their understanding of poetry, their courage, and their skill with spear and bow. And if the tests were passed, the young men and their families severed the most fundamental tie of that age. In Ireland, injury done to one's kin required vengeance by the family, but the families of the Fianna for-

In the Elf King's dark tower, Childe Rowland
found his sister, and there he battled for her life.

mally renounced all claims to revenge if the recruits were killed or injured; once the young men had joined the brotherhood, their comrades in the Fianna assumed the role of seeking out and getting satisfaction for any harm done to them.

Their manner of life became the stuff of legend. In summer, they roamed the country, living by the hunt, sleeping under the sky on the "three beddings of the Fianna" — branches, rushes and moss — bathing in streams, eating at campfires and listening to the songs of their own minstrels and the stories of their own bards. In winter, their quarters were among ordinary folk or in the fortresses of their chiefs.

The Fianna's greatest glory came under the leadership of Finn Mac Cumal, a man of such character that his name lived on the breath of Ireland's poets for centuries after his death. Finn was the bravest of them, it was said, and the wisest, for he had tasted a salmon whose flesh contained the wisdom of the world. He was the finest of their huntsmen, the best of their poets, the most just of judges. In a country where unstinting generosity was the mark of a man, Finn was the most generous of men: If the autumn leaves falling from the trees had turned to gold and the foam on the sea to silver, sang the bards, Finn would have given them all away.

Finn's greatness and his fidelity were echoed and returned by the warriors of the Fianna. Among his hearth companions were his son Oisin, the sweet singer, and his grandson Oscar, the fair. Diarmuid, the handsomest and kindest of men, was in his company. One-eyed Goll of Connacht, after Finn the best of the men of the Fianna, was there, and so too was Caoilte, a thin, gray man who could outrun the wind. They and their fellows were like sons and brothers to Finn. They were in his care and he in theirs.

Among them, Caoilte seemed to have the gentlest heart. It was not that he lacked ferocity or courage: In his youth, it was said, he had battled and killed a five-headed giant and slain an enchanted boar that none of his companions could touch. But he also had a curious kinship with the things of nature. He loved the secret life in the world, and this, it seemed, gave him certain powers over it. He had, for instance, an understanding of which herbs healed, which gave knowledge and which inspired love. So acute was his hearing that he could tell from the sound of a hunt in a forest how many packs of hounds there were and what prey they pursued — deer or hares or boars or badgers. And he could do more than simply listen, in the service of his leader:

It happened during Finn's time that the Fianna were becoming restless. They were a highly trained army, and in periods of idleness they sometimes became rebellious or fought with one or another of the factions that divided the lesser Irish Kings. To discourage this and to demonstrate his power, the High King of Ireland one summer had Finn seized and imprisoned in his fortress on the Hill of Tara.

News of the deed reached Caoilte in Finn's stronghold on the Hill of Allen, high above the Leinster marshes, and the warrior, outraged at the insult, headed south toward the High King's lands. He satisfied his anger by killing the High King's farmers in their huts and burning their fields, but this did not free his chief; and when Caoilte's first fury died, he entered the fortress of Tara itself. He made his way into the King's twelve-doored banqueting hall by the simple ruse of subduing the door guard and taking the man's clothes for a disguise. And so that night, Caoilte stood in the hall undetected, holding a tallow candle, as if he were one of the countless menials whose duty this was.

Hearth fire and candlelight gleamed on the shields that hung on the painted walls; it shone on the reddened faces of the King's men, seated in rows at the feasting benches. Caoilte made his way through the throng of serving men and jugglers, harpers and bards, to the end of the hall, where the High King's own bench was. Then he saw his chief, seated with honor, but humiliatingly shackled and under guard. Attracted by his movement, the King glanced at Caoilte — and glanced again. He knew Finn's companions well.

"I think I see your man Caoilte's eyes in that candle flame," said the King, nodding in the warrior's direction.

"He is a man of high deeds," Finn said. "He does not carry candles like a servant."

But Caoilte, in his anger at seeing his chief a captive, betrayed himself. "Tell me how I can gain my master's freedom," he said, lowering the tall candlestick and staring directly into the King's eyes.

Entertained by the man's audacity — and by his courage in coming alone to this well-defended hall — the High King considered the matter. At length he said, "The Fianna is unruly enough; show me orderly command. Bring me two of every wild beast that lives in Ireland. Bring them to me here, together and alive."

"No man can do this thing," said Finn.

"I will do it for my master's sake," said Caoilte. Without further comment, he set the candle down and strode from the hall.

He was gone for the end of summer and the beginning of autumn. The King's runners brought reports of him — of how he moved through the north, along the seacoast, into the great lochs, how he was seen in the mountains and in the branchy woods of the valleys, how he dared the deep gorges and caves. Finally, word came that he was returning to Tara and the High King's hall. Guards were posted along the five great roads that led across the plain to the whitewashed ramparts of the fortress on the hill. These men were the first to bring the reports of Caoilte's progress. Their accounts were delivered with barely suppressed laughter.

When Caoilte came within view of the ramparts, all could see what had caused the guards' reactions. Along the stone road the warrior strode, tall and reed-slender, his hair as gray as the winter sea. All about him, scampering and waddling, leaping and trotting, squawking and singing and growling and grunting, a shapeless, tatterdemalion company marched on Tara. Close by Caoilte's ankles, a pair of otters humped along, eyes bright with curiosity; hares hopped beside them, meandering off from time to time, only to be called back sharply by the war-

Two of every bird and beast in Ireland—brought to his hall—was
what the High King asked for freeing Finn Mac Cumal. Finn's
warrior Caoilte paid the price, all for love of his leader.

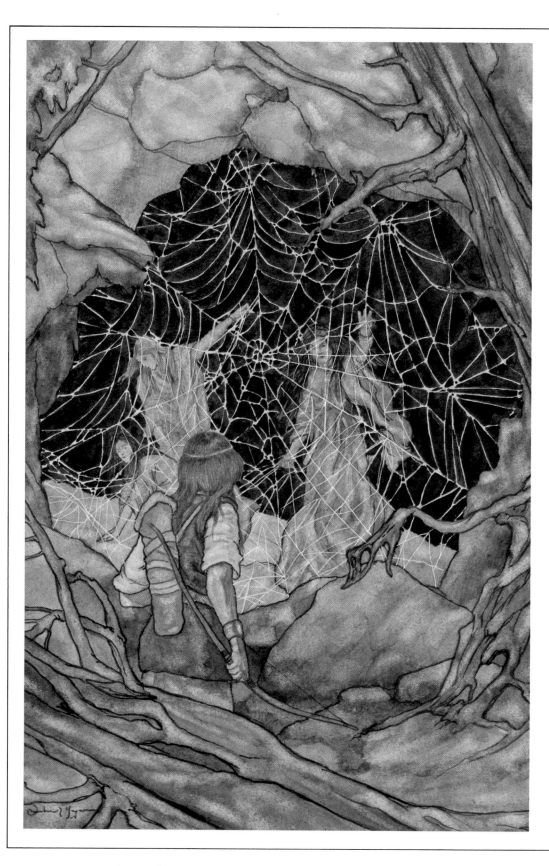

Finn Mac Cumal and his men once ventured into fairy territory and
were trapped in a web of weakness by three cave hags. A member of the
company eluded the net, however, and he would rescue his brothers-in-arms.

rior. Two sullen cats were there, and two badgers, low to the ground. Wolves loped ahead as a vanguard; skittish deer trotted at the flanks; a straggling line of cows and pigs and sheep brought up the rear. In his hands, Caoilte held two flapping wood ducks by the legs. And overhead flew every bird of Ireland—owls and swans, gulls and thrushes, blackbirds and nightingales, goldfinches and swallows, stonechats and cormorants and lapwings.

Along the road the animals swarmed, crowding into unruly heaps as they poured through Tara's gates and into the banqueting hall. The noise was deafening.

The High King stood in his hall with Finn beside him. Although he had been defeated, he too was laughing.

"Caoilte's rabble," he said finally.

"Look well, lord, and free my master. The terms are met this moment."

"He is free."

"Now, go," Caoilte shouted. He released the wood ducks, which flapped into the rafters of the hall, quacking dismally. The other birds rose in a whirlwind; the animals stampeded for the doors, clawing, scratching and biting as they went. Within moments, the hall was empty, except for a liberal blanket of droppings and puddles and a scattering of fur clumps and fallen feathers. From the courtyard outside came shouts and squeals as the High King's people ran from the wild things.

How Caoilte had done the deed, no one could tell, and he would not speak about it except to say that it had been tiresome. But his story was often told in Finn's own hall to amuse the men on winter nights when the cold blasts blew outside. It was a good-natured story, and the magic in it was untainted by evil or by real danger.

Most of the adventures of the men of the Fianna were darker far than Caoilte's tale. The Fianna lived in an age when the fairy race called the Side still held sway in kingdoms under Ireland's green hills or beneath the cold seas that lapped her shores. This elvish people, mighty in enchantment, watched the doings of the Irishmen with sharp and ancient eyes. The old ones were capricious: Sometimes they fought in league with the Fianna. Some of their women loved mortal men: The wife of Finn's youth and the mother of his son Oisin had been a daughter of the Side; Finn's man Diarmuid had loved a fairy woman; Caoilte's wife was said to be of the old race. More often, however, the elvish folk were enemies, lying in wait for unwary warriors. They might appear at any moment to trap mortals and drag them out of the sunlight into the ancient dark.

Such an entrapment happened once on the mountain called Ceiscoran, by the plains of Magh Chonaill in Connacht. On a day in high summer, Finn had called a hunt, and so exuberant were the huntsmen and the hounds as they sped across the meadow into the mountain forest that, the chroniclers said, they broke the peace of the countryside: "The deer were roused in their wild places and the badgers in their holes and the foxes in their wanderings and the birds on the wing."

Other beings were awakened, too. Finn and his men paused when they reached the forest, dismounting to drink from a brook.

*Fighting alone in aid of his fellows, Goll of Connacht faced the
power of old magic and earned his honor name: the "Flame of Battle."*

Finn saw a movement in the shadows, and he went to investigate. A strange sight awaited him in the undergrowth. A cave opened in the mountainside, its mouth covered with a webbing of coarse yarn. Three lumpish forms crouched there – old women whose matted hair fell over ashen faces. Their eyes were reddened and, it seemed, blind; spittle collected at the corners of their loose lips. They paid Finn no heed, being occupied by the yarn they were spinning with spindles that were no more than leafless holly branches.

Finn retreated and gathered his men. The company moved forward then and saluted the hags, eyeing the women and their work with curiosity.

"Peace be with you, mothers," Finn said. But the old women shook their heads and mumbled and went on with their spinning. Finn reached out a hand to the webbing that covered the mouth of the cave. The moment he plucked at it, a change came over him. His strong features trembled; his color faded; he sank to the ground and lay in the dirt, curled like an infant in the cradle and whimpering in an infant's voice. And one by one, as if helpless to resist, his men followed him and touched the hags' webbing and fell to the ground. Caoilte was among them, and Diarmuid, and Finn's son Oisin.

Only Goll, the one-eyed fighter, Finn's right hand, was not there. He had lingered on the plain below the mountain, and he arrived in the forest an hour later, attracted by the calling of the hunters' hounds.

The scene that met his eyes was fearsome. At the mouth of the cave, the hounds whined and cried; just inside were his leader and his companions, bound with cocoon-like strands of yarn. The men lay as if dead. Around them, gibbering and hissing, danced three black-robed figures armed with great swords. When Goll gave a shout, they turned. With battle shrieks, they made for him, and they seemed to swell and grow taller as they advanced.

Goll, called the "Flame of Battle," did not flinch. He dropped the hunting spears he carried, drew his own sword, and stood his ground. Grunting, the hags circled him. He turned swiftly, keeping them in sight of his one eye. Two moved to the right, but before they disappeared from his field of vision, Goll struck, slashing with the sword. It bit through the neck of one of the creatures and through the neck of the next. Headless, the two fell to the ground, nightmarish heaps of spouting blood and twitching muscle. Goll had no time to observe them. A weight slammed into his back. Spider-like arms and legs closed around him, and a foul crooning sounded in his ear.

He dropped his sword and gripped the arms, but he could not pry them loose. He staggered past the cave mouth toward the trees and slammed his burden against a trunk. The arms maintained their hold. Then Goll fell backward to the ground. With a gasp, the hag finally relinquished her grip. Goll leaped up, took his enemy by the hair and dragged her toward the cave. With leather straps from a shield that lay there, he bound the hag and laid her down by her headless sisters. Then he picked up his sword.

"Hold, champion, strong man that never went back in battle," the hag whined. Goll eyed the creature warily.

"I put my life in your protection. I swear by the gods of my people that I will give you Finn and the Fianna back if you spare me, and that they will be whole again."

"Free them, then," said Goll.

She began to chant in words he did not know. As the voice droned on, the strands that covered Finn and the others melted and fell away, and the men rose from the ground. Goll gave a shout to his brothers and cut the straps that bound the hag. Without another word, she crawled toward the edge of the clearing. The headless trunks shuddered to their knees and crawled with her, their heads bumping bloodily along the ground beside, and all three vanished into the shadows.

What the hags were, the chroniclers disputed. Some said they were soldiers of the Side who ruled that place and that they had been sent to end the disturbance the hunters caused. Others said that they were the Morrigan, the ancient goddess of death and war, who sometimes appeared in the form of three hags and sometimes in the form of three beautiful women and sometimes as black ravens. The Morrigan thirsted for human blood, and in those days, when her power and worship were long ended, she took it like a thief in the night when she saw the chance.

Whatever the hags' identity, Goll had defeated the creatures and saved his leader and his fellow warriors. And as long as the Fianna stood together, they triumphed in this way over the old ones.

But the Fianna did not always stand together, and their adversaries were not always the Side. In time, dissension corrupted the brotherhood's devotion. Bred for fighting, they were quarrelsome men. Diarmuid and Finn became enemies over a woman, and Diarmuid died through Finn's own wish. Goll fought with one of Finn's sons and killed the youth; when he heard that Finn sought revenge, the warrior lay on the rocks by the sea and willed himself to death. Oisin vanished into the world of the Side, drawn by the love of a fairy woman, and Finn never saw his son again.

In the end, the remnants of the Fianna grew rebellious and tried to take the High King's power for themselves. They joined with the troops of a minor Irish King and revolted, and they were defeated by the High King's forces. Those who survived drifted away to places of safety.

The warriors died one by one, until only Caoilte was left to sing of the Fianna and Finn Mac Cumal in the days of glory. It was said that when at last Caoilte was alone, old and ill, bereft of his sons and his companions, he left the mortals' world and went to live among the Side.

No one knew whether this was true. But a man who was High King of Ireland many centuries after the Fianna disappeared often told how he was stopped in a dark wood once on a moonless night. A tall, lean, gray man appeared out of the gloom and put his hands on the King's bridle.

"I am the King's candle bearer," said the wraith with a smile. "I was with Finn once." And then he vanished, the last of the brotherhood, still telling his love.

A Slave Maiden's Eye for Evil

The men and women of centuries past had few weapons to defend against spell-empowered evil, but clear wits, watchfulness and loyalty to one another were sometimes sufficient, as a Persian story tells: The tale was named for a man called Ali Baba, who lived in a village in the Elburz Mountains and maintained a meager existence by cutting wood in the dense forests that surrounded his village. He had a brother, Kassim, a merchant who had married well and kept a house of many rooms and many courtyards. Neither the poor brother nor the rich was the true hero of the tale, however. That role belonged to one of Kassim's slaves, a woman named Morgiana: She was a shrewd and handsome maiden, tireless in her devotion to the household she served.

The events of the story began in an oak forest a few hours' ride from the village. Rarely did people pass among those dark trunks and tangled boughs. Some said the place was haunted, some that it was the lair of wolfish *karkadanns*, the unicorns of the region. Ali Baba nevertheless rode his bony mule into the wood one afternoon, tethered the beast, and set to work with his ax. Sensing danger in the place, he looked around nervously each time leaves rustled or a branch creaked. But he had no real cause for alarm until he moved to a clearing where thickets

Faithful Morgiana, slave to Kassim and Ali Baba, closely guarded her household.

butted against a wall of mountain rock. Then the ground rumbled, thunder sounded through the trees, and the underbrush hissed and crackled. Dropping his load of kindling, Ali Baba swarmed up a tree and hid among the shuddering branches.

In moments, the clearing beneath him was crowded with armed, long-robed riders astride horses streaked with foam and weighed down with bulging saddlebags. Their leader threw back his hood to show a saturnine face, bristling of brow and black of beard. At his sign, the men dismounted and lifted the saddlebags from the horses. The leader pointed at the stone slab and said loudly, "Open, Sesame!"

A crack swept up the rock face and quickly widened. With a groan, a door opened into blackness. The chief of the company strode through this portal and disappeared, and in an orderly file, his men followed. When the last had vanished, the rock closed and became once more a seamless slab.

How long Ali Baba remained hidden in the tree, he never afterward could tell. But before he could gather his courage to move, the rock parted again, and the company issued from the darkness and mounted the waiting animals. The last man turned as he left and cried, "Close!" The rock slab obeyed.

After the hoofbeats had faded, Ali Baba climbed down from his perch. He stared at the slab. Then, to his own surprise, he pointed at it and said, "Open, Sesame!" As it had for the horsemen, the rock opened, releasing a gust of chill air. He peered into the fissure. Nothing moved. Small points of light shone in the shadows. He slipped into a vaulted cavern, and the rock closed behind him.

In the lamplight, anonymous lumps at his feet formed themselves into chests, bales and baskets, from which spilled

While Ali Baba watched from hiding, the brigand chief opened a door with a magic word.

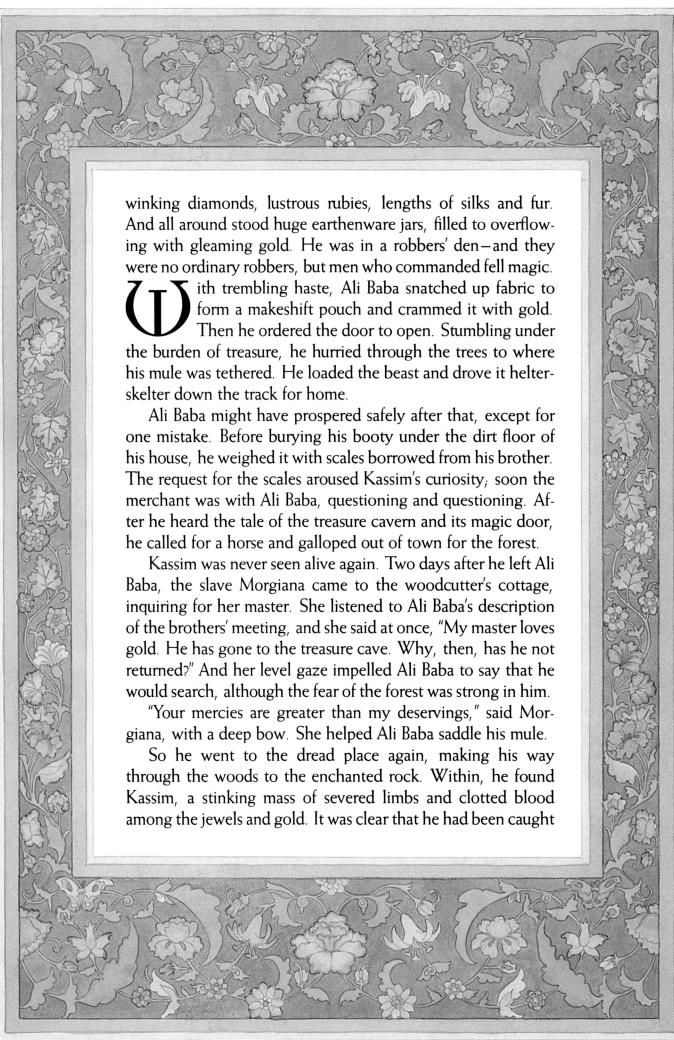

winking diamonds, lustrous rubies, lengths of silks and fur. And all around stood huge earthenware jars, filled to overflowing with gleaming gold. He was in a robbers' den—and they were no ordinary robbers, but men who commanded fell magic.

With trembling haste, Ali Baba snatched up fabric to form a makeshift pouch and crammed it with gold. Then he ordered the door to open. Stumbling under the burden of treasure, he hurried through the trees to where his mule was tethered. He loaded the beast and drove it helter-skelter down the track for home.

Ali Baba might have prospered safely after that, except for one mistake. Before burying his booty under the dirt floor of his house, he weighed it with scales borrowed from his brother. The request for the scales aroused Kassim's curiosity; soon the merchant was with Ali Baba, questioning and questioning. After he heard the tale of the treasure cavern and its magic door, he called for a horse and galloped out of town for the forest.

Kassim was never seen alive again. Two days after he left Ali Baba, the slave Morgiana came to the woodcutter's cottage, inquiring for her master. She listened to Ali Baba's description of the brothers' meeting, and she said at once, "My master loves gold. He has gone to the treasure cave. Why, then, has he not returned?" And her level gaze impelled Ali Baba to say that he would search, although the fear of the forest was strong in him.

"Your mercies are greater than my deservings," said Morgiana, with a deep bow. She helped Ali Baba saddle his mule.

So he went to the dread place again, making his way through the woods to the enchanted rock. Within, he found Kassim, a stinking mass of severed limbs and clotted blood among the jewels and gold. It was clear that he had been caught

Kassim, brother to Ali Baba, found the brigands' treasure cave — and died there.

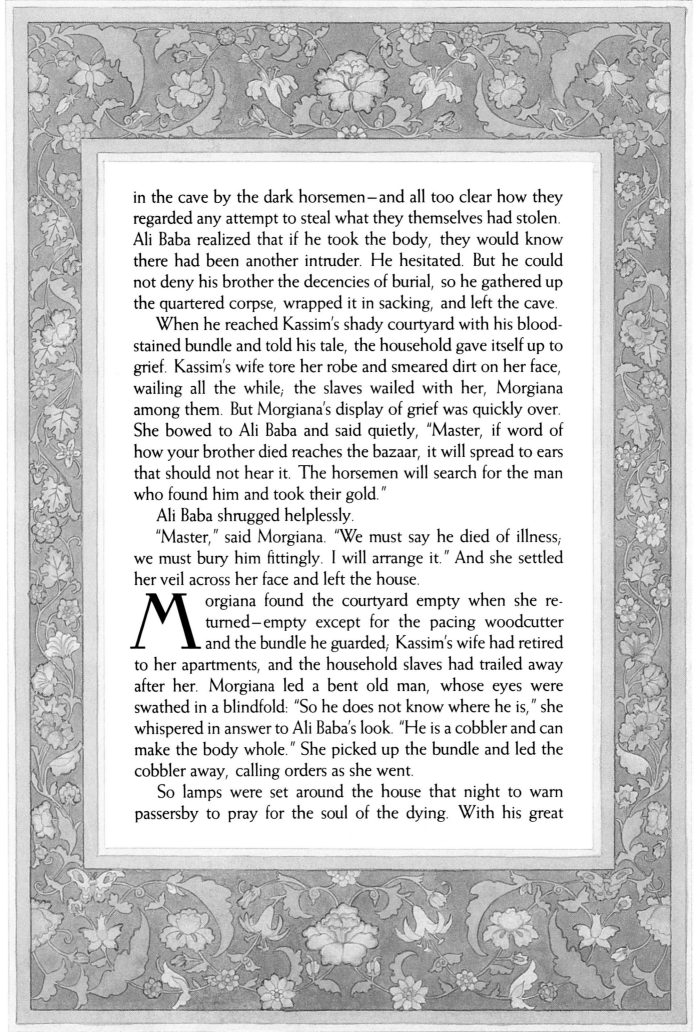

in the cave by the dark horsemen — and all too clear how they regarded any attempt to steal what they themselves had stolen. Ali Baba realized that if he took the body, they would know there had been another intruder. He hesitated. But he could not deny his brother the decencies of burial, so he gathered up the quartered corpse, wrapped it in sacking, and left the cave.

When he reached Kassim's shady courtyard with his blood-stained bundle and told his tale, the household gave itself up to grief. Kassim's wife tore her robe and smeared dirt on her face, wailing all the while; the slaves wailed with her, Morgiana among them. But Morgiana's display of grief was quickly over. She bowed to Ali Baba and said quietly, "Master, if word of how your brother died reaches the bazaar, it will spread to ears that should not hear it. The horsemen will search for the man who found him and took their gold."

Ali Baba shrugged helplessly.

"Master," said Morgiana. "We must say he died of illness; we must bury him fittingly. I will arrange it." And she settled her veil across her face and left the house.

Morgiana found the courtyard empty when she returned — empty except for the pacing woodcutter and the bundle he guarded; Kassim's wife had retired to her apartments, and the household slaves had trailed away after her. Morgiana led a bent old man, whose eyes were swathed in a blindfold: "So he does not know where he is," she whispered in answer to Ali Baba's look. "He is a cobbler and can make the body whole." She picked up the bundle and led the cobbler away, calling orders as she went.

So lamps were set around the house that night to warn passersby to pray for the soul of the dying. With his great

To save Ali Baba, Morgiana paid a cobbler to conceal the brigands' injuries to Kassim's body.

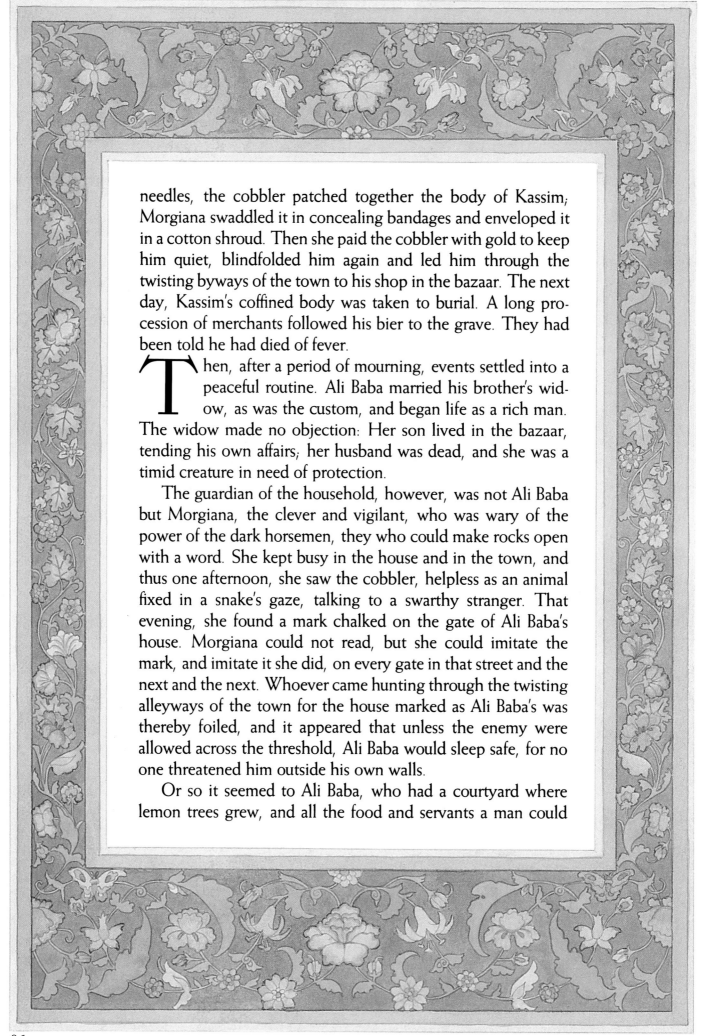

needles, the cobbler patched together the body of Kassim;
Morgiana swaddled it in concealing bandages and enveloped it
in a cotton shroud. Then she paid the cobbler with gold to keep
him quiet, blindfolded him again and led him through the
twisting byways of the town to his shop in the bazaar. The next
day, Kassim's coffined body was taken to burial. A long procession of merchants followed his bier to the grave. They had
been told he had died of fever.

Then, after a period of mourning, events settled into a
peaceful routine. Ali Baba married his brother's widow, as was the custom, and began life as a rich man.
The widow made no objection: Her son lived in the bazaar,
tending his own affairs; her husband was dead, and she was a
timid creature in need of protection.

The guardian of the household, however, was not Ali Baba
but Morgiana, the clever and vigilant, who was wary of the
power of the dark horsemen, they who could make rocks open
with a word. She kept busy in the house and in the town, and
thus one afternoon, she saw the cobbler, helpless as an animal
fixed in a snake's gaze, talking to a swarthy stranger. That
evening, she found a mark chalked on the gate of Ali Baba's
house. Morgiana could not read, but she could imitate the
mark, and imitate it she did, on every gate in that street and the
next and the next. Whoever came hunting through the twisting
alleyways of the town for the house marked as Ali Baba's was
thereby foiled, and it appeared that unless the enemy were
allowed across the threshold, Ali Baba would sleep safe, for no
one threatened him outside his own walls.

Or so it seemed to Ali Baba, who had a courtyard where
lemon trees grew, and all the food and servants a man could

Through the streets, Morgiana guided the cobbler, who was blindfolded as a precaution.

want, and a cache of golden coins in addition. He grew expansive with prosperity; a genial man, he acquired a reputation for generous hospitality in the months that followed Kassim's death. He was unsurprised—even pleased—when, in the late light of a summer evening, a traveler appeared at his gate leading a heavily burdened donkey train. This man said that he was an oil merchant come to sell his wares in the town. The inns were full, he said. Might he beg shelter from Ali Baba?

Ali Baba was glad to give it. He himself directed the unloading of the massive leather oil sacks; he sent his slaves scurrying with orders for a bath and for sherbet, cooled with mountain snow. He chattered to his visitor, rubbing his hands together and saying how his house was honored.

Morgiana watched this activity narrowly as she went about her work. The visitor was a man she had never seen before, tall and stooped, hawklike in profile and hooded of eye. She tugged at Ali Baba's sleeve and whispered, "Master, the horsemen have ways of finding what they want. Did you see this stranger in the forest?" But Ali Baba shook his head and chided her for discourtesy. He led his guest into the cool of the house, still chattering.

Unsatisfied, Morgiana crept at twilight into the walled kitchen courtyard where the oil sacks were stored. She touched one, and so heard a low voice within it.

"Is it time?" asked the voice.

"Not yet," she whispered quickly, and touched the next sack. Again she heard the query, and again she answered, "Not yet." In each sack was a man prepared to spring. The company of horsemen had invaded the house.

Morgiana's response was swift. She stepped into the kitchen

Robbed of his booty and the body of his victim Kassim, the brigand chief plotted revenge.

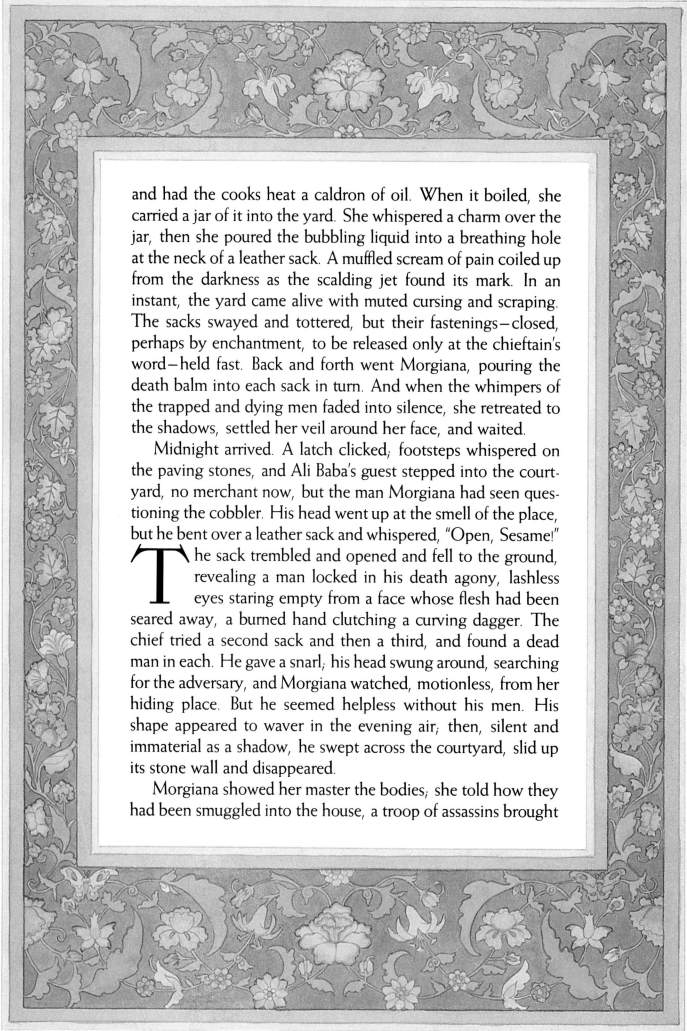

and had the cooks heat a caldron of oil. When it boiled, she carried a jar of it into the yard. She whispered a charm over the jar, then she poured the bubbling liquid into a breathing hole at the neck of a leather sack. A muffled scream of pain coiled up from the darkness as the scalding jet found its mark. In an instant, the yard came alive with muted cursing and scraping. The sacks swayed and tottered, but their fastenings—closed, perhaps by enchantment, to be released only at the chieftain's word—held fast. Back and forth went Morgiana, pouring the death balm into each sack in turn. And when the whimpers of the trapped and dying men faded into silence, she retreated to the shadows, settled her veil around her face, and waited.

Midnight arrived. A latch clicked; footsteps whispered on the paving stones, and Ali Baba's guest stepped into the courtyard, no merchant now, but the man Morgiana had seen questioning the cobbler. His head went up at the smell of the place, but he bent over a leather sack and whispered, "Open, Sesame!"

The sack trembled and opened and fell to the ground, revealing a man locked in his death agony, lashless eyes staring empty from a face whose flesh had been seared away, a burned hand clutching a curving dagger. The chief tried a second sack and then a third, and found a dead man in each. He gave a snarl; his head swung around, searching for the adversary, and Morgiana watched, motionless, from her hiding place. But he seemed helpless without his men. His shape appeared to waver in the evening air; then, silent and immaterial as a shadow, he swept across the courtyard, slid up its stone wall and disappeared.

Morgiana showed her master the bodies; she told how they had been smuggled into the house, a troop of assassins brought

In the shape of an oil merchant, the brigand chief sought Ali Baba's hospitality.

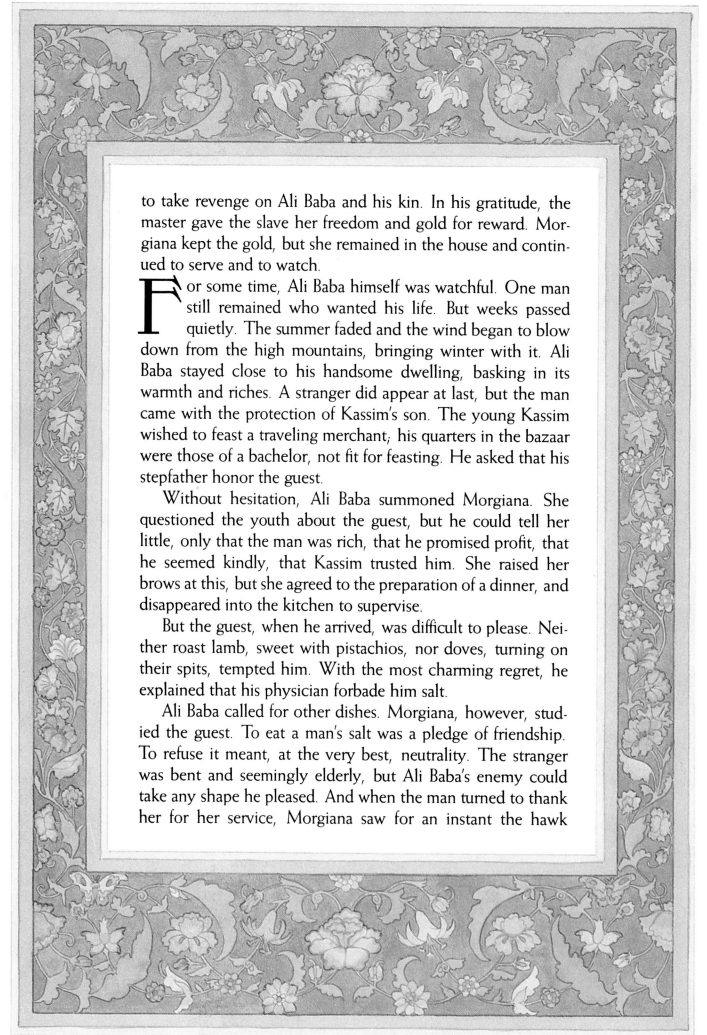

to take revenge on Ali Baba and his kin. In his gratitude, the master gave the slave her freedom and gold for reward. Morgiana kept the gold, but she remained in the house and continued to serve and to watch.

For some time, Ali Baba himself was watchful. One man still remained who wanted his life. But weeks passed quietly. The summer faded and the wind began to blow down from the high mountains, bringing winter with it. Ali Baba stayed close to his handsome dwelling, basking in its warmth and riches. A stranger did appear at last, but the man came with the protection of Kassim's son. The young Kassim wished to feast a traveling merchant; his quarters in the bazaar were those of a bachelor, not fit for feasting. He asked that his stepfather honor the guest.

Without hesitation, Ali Baba summoned Morgiana. She questioned the youth about the guest, but he could tell her little, only that the man was rich, that he promised profit, that he seemed kindly, that Kassim trusted him. She raised her brows at this, but she agreed to the preparation of a dinner, and disappeared into the kitchen to supervise.

But the guest, when he arrived, was difficult to please. Neither roast lamb, sweet with pistachios, nor doves, turning on their spits, tempted him. With the most charming regret, he explained that his physician forbade him salt.

Ali Baba called for other dishes. Morgiana, however, studied the guest. To eat a man's salt was a pledge of friendship. To refuse it meant, at the very best, neutrality. The stranger was bent and seemingly elderly, but Ali Baba's enemy could take any shape he pleased. And when the man turned to thank her for her service, Morgiana saw for an instant the hawk

Into leather oil sacks where the brigands were hiding, Morgiana poured boiling oil.

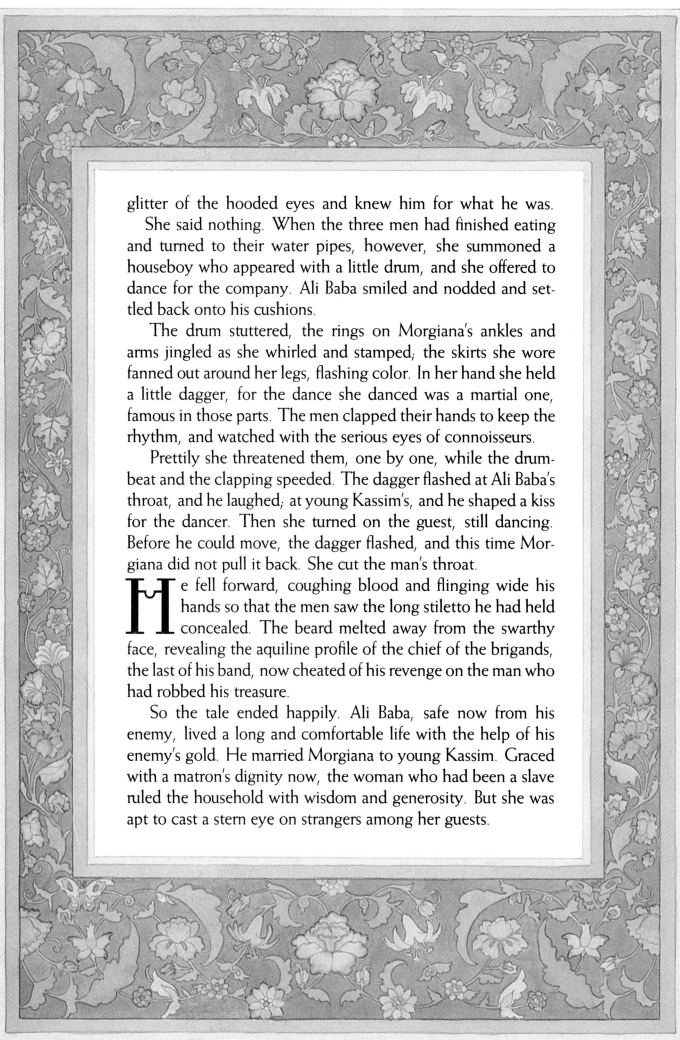

glitter of the hooded eyes and knew him for what he was.

She said nothing. When the three men had finished eating and turned to their water pipes, however, she summoned a houseboy who appeared with a little drum, and she offered to dance for the company. Ali Baba smiled and nodded and settled back onto his cushions.

The drum stuttered, the rings on Morgiana's ankles and arms jingled as she whirled and stamped; the skirts she wore fanned out around her legs, flashing color. In her hand she held a little dagger, for the dance she danced was a martial one, famous in those parts. The men clapped their hands to keep the rhythm, and watched with the serious eyes of connoisseurs.

Prettily she threatened them, one by one, while the drumbeat and the clapping speeded. The dagger flashed at Ali Baba's throat, and he laughed; at young Kassim's, and he shaped a kiss for the dancer. Then she turned on the guest, still dancing. Before he could move, the dagger flashed, and this time Morgiana did not pull it back. She cut the man's throat.

He fell forward, coughing blood and flinging wide his hands so that the men saw the long stiletto he had held concealed. The beard melted away from the swarthy face, revealing the aquiline profile of the chief of the brigands, the last of his band, now cheated of his revenge on the man who had robbed his treasure.

So the tale ended happily. Ali Baba, safe now from his enemy, lived a long and comfortable life with the help of his enemy's gold. He married Morgiana to young Kassim. Graced with a matron's dignity now, the woman who had been a slave ruled the household with wisdom and generosity. But she was apt to cast a stern eye on strangers among her guests.

Skirts flying, dagger flashing, Morgiana danced for Ali Baba's enemy – and wove his doom.

Chapter Three

Strong Arms, Sturdy Hearts

Gawain of Orkney, King Arthur's knight, was the flower of chivalry: The Welsh called him Gwalch-mei, or "Falcon of May," and Gwalchgivy, meaning "White Falcon," to honor his valor. When he was in his prime, it was said, the sun itself smiled on him. Yet Gawain was no more than a man, and like other men, he was vulnerable to the magic wielded by the beings of the first world. Once, he was entrapped in a spell for no reason greater than denying the ancient ones the honor they demanded.

Gawain's adventure occurred in the course of a quest: With thirty of Arthur's knights, he had traveled to Brittany in search of Merlin the Enchanter. The aged adviser to the King had vanished—into the hands of elder powers, it was said. After some weeks, the company of knights separated, fanning out across the countryside to look for the wizard. Alone, Gawain entered the forest of Brocéliande. It seemed to him that this great wood, a bastion of the old world still looming in the new, might hold the man he sought. A haunted place, Brocéliande was full of murmurings, of eyes that watched intruders and of invisible guardians that followed them.

But on this summer morning the wood was quiet. The great trees drowsed, and even the watchful birds were silent. The only sounds Gawain heard were what any rider might hear: the creaking of his saddle, the dull clinking of his horse's bridle and the rustle of the undergrowth beneath its hoofs. So Gawain rode easily, locked in his own thoughts and paying less attention to his surroundings than he ought.

He hardly noticed how the morning wore on, and he failed to remark when the shafts of sunlight that pierced the leaf canopy became vertical columns. It was noontide, a time that escaped definition, being neither morning nor afternoon—an in-between time like midnight, when beings of the other world were free to roam.

And indeed, one wandered near the narrow track where Gawain rode, flitting among the tree trunks and in and out of the columns of light. She was a tall young creature, pale and slender as a birch, clothed in a trailing gown of green that fluttered around her as lightly as leaves in the wind. So colored by the forest was she that she might have been a tree spirit, released from a tree's rooted stillness to dance in the midday sun. Gawain's horse tossed its head and whickered at the sight. But Gawain rode on, oblivious.

A small, bell-like voice halted him: "Sir! You did not greet me, and you are riding through my own hall." He looked around him then, and saw the fairy woman where she stood by the track, quite at home among the trees.

"Lady," he said, "I did not see you."

In return, she gave him a ruler's glance, cool and thoughtful. This was followed by a sudden smile.

"Is it so? Not fitting for a knight of Arthur's. It seems you need schooling in courtesy," said the fairy.

Gawain waited. He knew there was little chance of averting the power of an old one in this forest.

"You may live another life, until you prove you know what is due my kind," the forest woman said. Then she vanished among the leaves.

"What life?" asked Gawain of the air.

"That of the creature you next encounter," it answered.

These were ominous words, for who knew what waited in the forest? Gawain might be condemned by the fairy's enchantment to live as a badger in the earth or a water rat in the mud of a stream, or as hunters' prey—boar, hare or deer. He had no choice, however, but to fare forward and so discover his fate.

This Gawain did, and his fate came upon him soon enough. Not far along the track, on a stone beside it, sat a dwarf, a squat and crooked creature with bandy legs and a thickened body. He squinted up at Gawain, his black eyes set deep in a seamed and leathery face. That was all Gawain saw before the world exploded. His skull and chest tightened intolerably; his fingers flexed and curled; hot pain coursed through his legs. Overhead the leaves wheeled sickeningly. His vision blurred and darkened.

When it cleared, he found himself sitting on the dirt track staring down at his own short, bowed legs. Averting his eyes from them, he scrambled to his feet. From his throat came an unfamiliar, tinny squeak: "Am I a dwarf, then, fit to be no more than a courtier's toy?"

"My lord, you are. Truly, I grieve for you. I suffered this enchantment too, and now it is by your misfortune that I am released." This answer came from a young man who stood beside Gawain, looking down—a fine young man, gently born, by his bearing.

Gawain sighed. "Do you know of King Arthur and his court?" he asked.

"I do," said the stranger.

"Then go to the King in my name. Say what has happened, and bid him not search for me. I will return, if I can find the act that will free me from the spell." The young man hesitated, for he was unwilling to leave a fellow warrior in such a plight. Then he nodded by way of salute and strode off down the track, toward the world where humankind ruled.

Gawain turned toward his horse. It too had shrunk, until it was no larger than the shaggy ponies he had ridden across his windswept island home as a small boy. With his stubby legs, it was difficult for Gawain to mount even that small a steed. But he scrambled into the saddle at last and spurred the animal deeper into Bro-

An enchantress's wrath transformed Sir Gawain into a dwarf and made a pony of his battle charger. To undo the spell, Gawain had to show he possessed a full measure of knightly merit despite his diminutive form.

céliande, where some test must wait. He knew no other course to take.

For a long time, the forest ignored him. He traveled steadily, pausing only to drink from a stream or hunt for food. By night, he slept under trees so dense with leaves that no glimmer of stars was visible. Not a soul did he see, and even the air was still, so that the leaves hung perfectly motionless from dawn to dusk.

But Gawain was a man under an enchantment, and as if that condition made him visible to others caught in the coils of the elder world, he attracted the attention of another being in the same plight. He rode seven days in all. At twilight on the seventh, he dismounted at a brook to water the pony. Heavy-branched oaks formed a canopy above the whispering water. From their leaves, a sigh drifted.

"Hail, stranger." The words hung mournfully in the air.

"Who speaks?" said Gawain.

"Merlin the Enchanter, he who made Arthur King of all Britain."

"Lord Merlin, I am Gawain. Only show yourself to me," the dwarf cried. He peered among the oaks but could discern no sign of the wizard. The voice had come from one of the trees, it seemed.

There was a note of wry amusement in the voice when it replied: "Sir Gawain, only show yourself to me."

Gawain paused, silenced. Merlin continued: "Tell the King that the old ones have me. By their spells I am captive in

The test of Gawain's valor came in the form of two rogue
knights. Although no larger than a child, he challenged them
to combat, thus displaying the courage of the bravest of men.

this oak and ever shall be. Tell him to beware of fairy women, for it was one I loved who put me here."

"Lord, how can you return to us?"

"I never shall return," said Merlin, "and never speak again to men. Farewell, Gawain, last of my own kind to hear me."

Tears sprang to Gawain's eyes, for the voice had a dead ring: This was the end of all their searching. He swallowed, struggling for speech.

"If you would free yourself, Gawain, remember when the trial comes that you are a man," the faint voice said. When these words faded, the wind rose, so that the oak leaves rustled. Gawain touched the bark, but it was as rough and inert as any tree's; no human presence could he feel. At length, Gawain mounted the pony and took up his journey once more.

It lasted only another night and a morning. Then a high cry echoed through the wood. Gawain reined the pony in and heard the cry again. He followed it, and the sound led him into a small clearing, where an ugly scene confronted him.

In the clearing, her back against a tree, was a maiden. She was a charcoal burner's or woodsman's daughter, perhaps, because she wore a gray peasant's gown, much patched, and wooden clogs. Two knights – big, coarse, laughing men in battered mail and ragged tunics – flanked her. One clutched at her hair and the other at her dress. Peasant girls were often preyed upon by the landless knights who roamed the countryside then. The intentions of these men were obvious.

"Release her!" Gawain shouted in his shrill dwarf's voice. Turning quickly, the knights saw the challenger and let the maiden go. Here was better entertainment. They advanced on Gawain.

"Look at you, an ugly little toad in man's shape," said one.

"A pygmy knight mounted on a baby's horse," said the other. "Now, little fellow, you must be taught not to annoy your betters." And with a swinging blow of his fist, he knocked Gawain from the saddle. The pony bolted.

Stunned, the dwarf lay on the ground with dirt in his mouth and laughter rolling high over his head. An iron foot cracked into his side, and the laughter redoubled. The foot struck again, and the rage and shame in the dwarf's heart gave way to cold, cunning fury. Gawain rolled with the third kick, bounded to his feet, and swept his sword from its sheath.

His assailants grinned wolfishly then, their eyes alight with anticipation. But when they closed in, Gawain was ready.

Where does the dwarf strike who fights a giant? Where he can: Gawain stabbed at one knight's unprotected thigh just above the greave; his dwarf arms drove the blade easily through heavy muscle to grate against the bone. The man gave a scream of surprise and pain and fell back against his companion. Instantly, the dwarf struck again, grazing the belly of the other man. Then, leaping back out of range, Gawain began to circle, waiting for an opening.

The knights had the longer reach, but they were large and slow, and they had looked for brutish sport, not for a true fight. Gawain darted at them again and again, wielding his sword like a stiletto and easily evading their clumsy efforts to scythe him down.

Suddenly, a clear voice sounded: "That will do; the trial is finished. The dwarf possesses the courage of a man and the heart of a falcon."

The knights simply vanished, and Gawain was left staring at the empty air.

The words came from the woman the knights had been tormenting. But she had changed. No poor peasant now, she was the green-gowned fairy Gawain had met before. "Brave knight," she said, "the maidens' defense. We of my kind will remember and call on you when we have need. And you will remember also what powers we have and what is due us."

The knight bowed to her where she stood among her trees. At once, he was himself again, tall and straight—and alone in the clearing.

In this way, his adventure ended. It had been a strange, almost contradictory encounter with the other world. Yet it was typical of that age and that stage of relations between mortals and the fairy race.

Powerful and jealous of their waning power, prone to give and take according to whims no mortal could predict or control, the beings of the first world alternately aided and attacked their human successors. The challenges of the old ones were, in fact, tests of human character, trials of the younger race's fiber. Possession of the planet hung in the balance. For humankind to maintain its newly gained hold on the earth required the best that men and women could offer—not only the valor of a Gawain, but determination, the intelligence to discover what defensive action averted or undid enchantment, and the courage to perform that action.

In most cases, these tests were individual affairs, sometimes taking place on small farms and in isolated villages, among the humble folk of the world. The British, for instance, were fond of telling the tale of Thumbling. He was the son of a farm couple who had so desired a child that they wished for one, "even if he were no bigger than a thumb." Wishing aloud was rash in those days, given the presence of magic in the world. The fairies overheard the couple's wish, and nine months afterward, Thumbling was born. A product of fairy malice, he never grew taller than three inches.

The child was nevertheless beloved by his parents, and what he lacked in stature he made up for in wit and courage. He directed his father's cart horse by standing within the curve of the animal's ear and shouting instruction in his tiny voice. A traveling juggler observed this activity one day, said the storytellers, and offered to buy the boy to exhibit him at fairs. At Thumbling's urging, his father made the sale—for a handsome sum—and the juggler carried the boy away in his hat. But Thumbling escaped from the man by scurrying into a mousehole that led into a cottage and thence into a neighboring barn, where he took shelter. Within a few days, he had journeyed alone through the fields and arrived home again, having earned his grateful parents a small for-

*Taking refuge in the mouseholes and shadowed crannies of houses
and barns, a fairy-made boy named Thumbling—tiny in size but
great in heart—escaped those who sought to exploit him as a freak.*

Some of the old ones of the earth rewarded mortals who revered them.
German maidens found that if they sweetly obeyed the spinning fairy
known as Mother Holle, she might shower them with gold.

tune by the fairy's curse that shaped him.

Other tales told of village children dealing directly with creatures of the other world. In Thuringia and Lower Saxony, for instance, people spoke of Mother Holle, half old goddess, half fairy, sometimes friendly to humankind and sometimes not. She was the patroness of spinning and protected the cultivation of flax, but she also stole unbaptized infants from their cradles. Some people said that Mother Holle rode the skies and that snowfalls occurred when she shook out her feather beds; others thought that wells and fountains were the portals to a subterranean world where she ruled. Those who ventured there and pleased her might find themselves rewarded with showers of gold; but those who irritated her could emerge maimed or filth-covered.

Creatures such as the sharp-eared spirits who made Thumbling into a tiny manikin, or Mother Holle, interfering with the activities of villagers, were isolated beings. And tales of village folk—of miniature tricksters and good children who pleased the fairies—were but small incidents in a greater battle that continued century after century and could involve whole kingdoms. When human rulers fought with the creatures of Faerie, all their people might suffer.

Such a conflict happened once in the southwest of Wales, at a time when the beings of the other world were still numerous and led by powerful lords. The unfolding of these events began in the kingdom of Dyfed, a place of high mountains and well-watered valleys, where the harvests were good and the people prosperous. And the beginning was a return.

One day, two men came home to Dyfed—two warriors weary and aching from old wounds. They had long been at war in Ireland, a war so devastating that only seven of their once-mighty company returned to Wales. The younger of the two was Dyfed's lord, Pryderi by name. The elder was Pryderi's kinsman, Manawyddan, son of Llyr.

What these men wanted now was peace. Pryderi was eager to see his wife, Kigva. With Kigva in his fortress was Pryderi's mother, Rhiannon. She was a fairy woman who, years before, had left her people forever to marry Pryderi's father. Widowed now, she was beautiful still. Pryderi had promised her to Manawyddan, in token of his love for his brother-in-arms.

Through the bleak mountains of the north the two men trudged, down to river-laced lowlands. Autumn had settled on the land. The valleys were golden with grain; the apple trees bent with their burdens; in orchards and fields, the people of Dyfed busily gathered in the harvest. Pryderi was soon recognized, and word of his approach flew before him, from hamlet to hamlet. When the travelers turned at last onto the rolling road that led to Pryderi's stronghold, people gathered behind them and made a procession to cover the last familiar miles.

Pryderi's hilltop fortress was a formidable place, ringed with earthworks and palisades, but its great wooden gates stood open in welcome, and the smoke of feasting rose in ribbons from the halls within.

In the Welsh realm of Dyfed, two noble couples had the temerity to
trespass on Faerie. At once, thunder sounded and mist cloaked their world.

When the magic mist lifted, Dyfed was empty of animals and people. Seeing themselves alone, the four mortals—Pryderi and Manawyddan, and their wives, Kigva and Rhiannon—left the desolate kingdom and set out for England.

At the gates stood Kigva, straight and still, as befitted a lord's wife, but flushed with delight. Rhiannon was beside her. Silver-haired now, the older woman was yet as slender and flamelike as she had been in her youth: Those with fairy blood were kindly treated by age, it seemed, even when they had renounced their powers to dwell among men and women.

That day and the days after were joyful, unshadowed by any sense that a darkness was rising ahead. Rhiannon accepted Manawyddan for her new husband, as her son wished, and she was happy, for she had been long alone. The warrior was as white-haired as she, and he was a silent man, but he had about him a great gentleness that pleased her. As for Manawyddan, fresh from war and sorrow, he considered himself the most fortunate of men.

After the marriage, the two couples feasted and hunted and roamed the countryside of Dyfed. In that autumn, said the chroniclers, the land was especially rich—the rivers glittering with fish, the forests teeming with game. Carefree, savoring life's plenitude, the four lovers charmed Pryderi's court and his people. They were constant companions: Pryderi and Kigva, young and lively; Manawyddan and Rhiannon, smiling and serene.

One evening, however, when the feasting was finished and the servants were eating in their quarters, Manawyddan grew restless. "Lady," he said, with a smile at Rhiannon, "show me the door by which you entered this world."

"It is not safe, lord," Rhiannon replied.

The people of Faerie were alien to her now.

Her son Pryderi thought otherwise, however. He was on his feet at once, calling orders to the grooms, and it was not long before the couples left the warmth of the hall and rode to Gorsedd Arbeth—or "the Mound of Arbeth."

This was a low, grass-covered hill set among the trees of a wood that stretched away from Pryderi's fortress. It was unremarkable in appearance but charged with mystery: The people of Dyfed said that if a man of royal blood sat on the hill, he would receive either a terrible wound or see a great wonder, as if the touching of the earth there opened an invisible gate into another world. Indeed, on that hill, long years before, Pryderi's father had sat, and thereby summoned Rhiannon to dwell among humankind and share its fate.

The company rode up the hill and dismounted. All was still around them. In the distance, through the branches of the forest, the lamps of the fortress shone, and guards called quietly from the ramparts to mark the hour. Here, however, the life of the world seemed suspended. Moonlight silvered the grass and trees and glimmered on the hair of Rhiannon. The horses shook their bridles and side-stepped and blew long jets of steaming breath into the night air. This was no place for mortals.

"Come away, lord," said Rhiannon. "It is unsafe." Her voice seemed to crackle in the air. Manawyddan nodded then, and he signaled to Pryderi that they should leave. But before Pryderi could

speak, thunder rolled among the stars. As though in answer to the sound, mist coiled up from the ground, reaching pale fingers around the legs of the horses, closing over the riders. The moon and stars vanished; so thick was this mist that it hid Rhiannon from Manawyddan and Kigva from Pryderi. Manawyddan reached to catch his wife's hand. He said the others' names, and when they answered, he bade them stay where they were, lest one should be lost.

So the four waited, while the vaporous exhalation of another world boiled around them and the thunder rumbled in the sky. How long they remained there beside their sidling horses, none of them could say. At some point, the thunder's voice dropped, and the mist slowly receded until they stood above it, beneath a sky rosy with morning, and looked down on a sea of white. That too faded away as the sun rose and revealed their home to them.

But the Dyfed that lay under their eyes had been drained of human presence.

Reaching England, the exiles became craftsmen—shieldmakers, saddle makers, sewers of shoes. But the anger of the fairies followed them, it seemed: They were driven away from every English village and forced back to Dyfed once more.

"Where they had once seen their flocks and herds and dwellings," wrote the chroniclers, "they now saw nothing; no animal, no smoke, no fire, no man—only the houses of the court, deserted, uninhabited, without man or beast in them."

Without speaking, the four adventurers mounted their horses and rode down the slope of Gorsedd Arbeth, through the trees that divided it from Pryderi's stronghold, and into the fortress itself. No guard greeted them there; none of Pryderi's company awaited them. The fires were dead; the kitchens and stables and barracks and forges were empty. And seeing all this, they gathered in Pryderi's hall. Pryderi himself laid the hearth fire and lighted it, having no servants to summon. His companions warmed their hands at the flames and listened to the silence.

"What enemy have we set loose among us?" Pryderi asked his mother. But Rhiannon only shook her head. She had been separate from the beings of Faerie most of her life, and she knew nothing of their world or ways now.

"This is some spell. How can we lift it and find my people?" the son asked.

Rhiannon could not say. She did not know who had cast the spell or why. She did not know its terms. Helplessly, she turned to her husband, the oldest and the wisest of them.

"Let us wait for a sign," said Manawyddan in response. "I cannot fight an enemy I cannot see."

So they settled in the silent hall. They fared well enough. In those rough days, even the greatest were adept at the tasks of everyday. Kings were not strangers to stables and forges; queens sat at looms and wove cloth like other women. Now Pryderi and Manawyddan hunted and fished; Kigva and Rhiannon dressed and cooked the game. Sometimes they all rode out together, seeking other folk, but no folk dwelled in Dyfed.

After many months, when the winds blew cold on Arbeth and clawed at the fortress gates, when winter settled on the lonely hall and no sign came, Manawyddan said, "We must leave this place and travel in disguise, that the enemy may not follow us with his eyes."

They did that. The chroniclers say the four of them went into exile in England, traveling as craftsmen and their wives. In small villages they settled, in smoky little huts, and earned their bread as the common people did. It was said that first they set up as saddle makers and made blue-enameled saddles, more beautiful than any the English had seen; that next they made shields; then, when they had done, they made shoes, gleaming with gold. But it seemed that the eye of the enchanter who had enspelled Dyfed pursued the four on their wanderings, for they were driven from each village by the townsfolk as foreigners and competitors in trade.

When they were cast out for the third time, Manawyddan led them back into Dyfed. With grain-laden mules and a pack of hunting dogs, they journeyed across the border mountains, through villages whose fields lay untilled and whose houses stood open and deserted, to the fortress at Arbeth once more. As

In empty Dyfed, a splendid palace appeared, and this was the
next part of the pursuing spell. Manawyddan and Pryderi stumbled
upon it while hunting, and Pryderi was drawn across the threshold.

if they were leashed to it, the enchantment had forced them back to the place where its power was strongest.

They found the waiting fortress little changed. Dust lay thick on every bench and table. Winds had blown leaves across the floor of the hall and scattered the ashes from the central hearth. Foxes had nested in the kitchens and mice in the straw of the beds. When the women lifted the woven bedcovers, clouds of moths fluttered around their heads.

Homecoming, so splendid and joyful when Pryderi and Manawyddan came back from war, was now a prosaic matter of lighting the fire to drive away the damp, clearing the debris of empty seasons, storing the grain they had brought until the time should come for sowing, and housing the lean mules in the stables that once had held Pryderi's gleaming horses. When the first evening darkened, they brought their dogs in for warmth. Behind the hounds, the doors swung shut, gathering the wanderers home.

They lived by hunting, as they had done before, and the days passed uneventfully for a while. But they were close to their fairy foes now and in greater danger than they knew.

It happened that Pryderi and Manawyddan hunted one day with the dogs and cornered a white boar in a copse not far from the fortress. As the dogs snarled and barked, the beast turned at bay, its little eyes glittering red, its curving tusks gleaming. Pawing at the ground with sharp-edged hoofs, it squealed on a high, shrill note. The men approached for the kill, spears raised. But the boar backed and

swerved and then retreated before they could be certain of their aim. They pursued it to the edge of the wood, where boar and dogs disappeared among the trees.

The two men charged through the wood, and at its verge, where the trees began to thin, they saw a meadow that they did not recognize. In the meadow stood a palace—not a wooden fortress but a cluster of soaring spires built of sparkling stone. Its gate was open, and within the archway a fountain burbled. A massive golden bowl hung above the water. Pryderi strode toward the bowl, fascinated by its gleam, filled with a desire to touch the metal.

"Pryderi, do not go," the older man cried. "This place is not of men's making."

Pryderi did not reply; indeed, he seemed not even to hear. Puppet-like, he reached up to the bowl. Then he stood frozen, his hands sealed to the gold sides and his mouth working soundlessly.

Manawyddan did not leave Pryderi that afternoon. He waited near the gate, leaning on his spear and staring into the palace courtyard, as if to summon the enemy. No enemy came forth. As dusk fell, Rhiannon appeared, drawn perhaps by a mother's instinct.

"Where is my son?"

Manawyddan gestured, and Rhiannon turned on him, her gentleness lost. "You have been a bad companion, husband, and so have lost a good one," she said. Without another word, she ran toward the golden bowl. In an instant, it had trapped her; in another,

Within the fairy palace, Pryderi was held in thrall by a vessel of gold. Rhiannon, herself of the fairy race but tied to humankind, sought to rescue him and was trapped as well.

Ever wrathful toward the mortals, the King of the fairies sent an army of mice to
devour their grain. But Manawyddan chased the destroyers and captured one.

the thunder of enchantment sounded, and mist rose in the meadow. When the mist cleared, the palace was gone.

Later that night, Manawyddan returned alone to Kigva at Pryderi's fortress and told her his tale. She wailed with grief, then fell silent and watched him with frightened eyes. She was a timid woman, used to the company and command of her young husband, and she was alone now. It seemed to her that Manawyddan gazed on her with desire as he spoke, and she had no wish to warm an old man's bed.

But Manawyddan said, "Child, I will not harm you. You are my daughter, as you are Rhiannon's. We will wait together and find a way to free them."

"What shall we do?" Kigva asked. "How shall we live, two people alone in an empty land?"

"Plant," said Manawyddan. "It is the season."

And plant he did – three crofts of wheat, which grew with the seasons as it should. When the wheat stood tall and ripe for

harvest, the force of enchantment struck once more – this time at the human husband of the fairy woman and at the human wife of the fairy woman's son. A morning came when Manawyddan found one of the wheat fields stripped bare and all his work gone for nothing. He said little about this, other than to condemn thievery. But that night, he left Kigva alone by the hearth and mounted guard in the field.

In the small hours, he returned, waking Kigva. She watched while he suspended his leather glove from a soot-blackened beam. The glove twitched and danced in the air. "That glove is a prison for a mouse," said Manawyddan. "It was one of an army of thousands swarming through my grain, but it was fatter and slower than the others."

"Lord, what will you do with a mouse?"

"Hang it. That is the punishment for thieves."

"Lord, this is unworthy of your honor, to hang a mouse."

"Nevertheless, I shall hang it. It is the first soldier of my enemy that I have seen."

And at dusk of that day, Manawyddan

strode across the grainfield, through the woods and up the haunted slope of Gorsedd Arbeth to the invisible door of the enemy's domain, carrying the bulging glove, which had twine tied around its mouth to keep the prisoner penned. He set forked twigs into the dirt of the mound and placed a stick across them to serve as a crosspiece for his tiny scaffold.

"What have you there, lord?" a voice called out. Manawyddan looked up and saw an elderly scholar leaning on a staff. The man was dressed in the dark robes and hood of his calling, and his face could not be seen.

"Greetings," Manawyddan replied with a cold smile. "You are the first man other than my companions that I have seen here in seven years. How came you to Gorsedd Arbeth?"

"Why, I am passing by, on the way to

With the captured mouse as a hostage, Manawyddan bargained for the lives of
Rhiannon and Pryderi and for the health of his land. In the end, Dyfed was restored
and all things set again on the course that vengeful enchantment had turned askew.

my own country. What are you doing here on the hill?"

"Hanging a mouse," said Manawyddan. He gave the glove a vicious tweak.

"That is unworthy of such a lord as you," answered the scholar. "Let the poor beast go."

"Oh no. It is in my hand and I shall hang it."

"It is nothing to me, except for the cruelty. Here is silver for the mouse's life."

Manawyddan shook his head. He drew from his tunic a piece of twine and began to fashion a noose. The scholar watched him for some moments; then he sighed and walked away, mumbling to himself.

When he had gone, a priest appeared. The priest too talked with Manawyddan and offered money for the mouse, and he too was refused.

Finally, a man strode out of the gathering darkness toward the mound, a tall, grave man, clothed in the rich robes of a bishop or a ruler. When his offer for the mouse was refused, he said, "What, then, can I offer for the mouse's life? You have only to name your price."

Manawyddan rose and looked into the man's eyes, which were as gray as winter and as old as time. "This," the mortal said. "Pryderi and Rhiannon freed from your spell and Dyfed released from enchantment."

The other paused a moment in thought. "You have it," he said at last. "Now give me the mouse."

"I will release the beast when you tell me who you are and what it is."

"I am Llwyd, son of Kil Coed, of the people who gave Rhiannon birth. The enchantments I laid for her and her son were vengeance for the way she was taken from us to live among mortals, betraying her own kind and those who loved her. The mice were my people. The mouse you have is my own lady. She is slow because she is with child. Now give her to me."

"When you swear never to cast enchantment on Dyfed again. When you promise not to take revenge for my victory."

"I swear. And well for you that you made the demand, for revenge was in my mind. Now give me the mouse."

"When Rhiannon and Pryderi stand before me."

"They are here."

So they were, running toward Gorsedd Arbeth. Manawyddan loosened the glove, and a field mouse scampered clumsily out, making straight for the hands of Llwyd. When he touched it, the little beast vanished. A fairy woman stood in its place, trembling as she gazed on Manawyddan.

"Now, see your mortal world, come again to life," cried Llwyd. It was so. In the fields, flocks moved through the dusky light. Geese waddled toward the fortress with guardian children in their wake. All around, in the fortress and on the hillsides, lights blossomed – the waking hearth fires of the people.

Thus the enmity between the old beings and the new ended in Dyfed. One man had done it, one quiet man, working with no magic and no weapons, but with human patience only, and human intelligence, to secure mortal rule in his corner of the world.

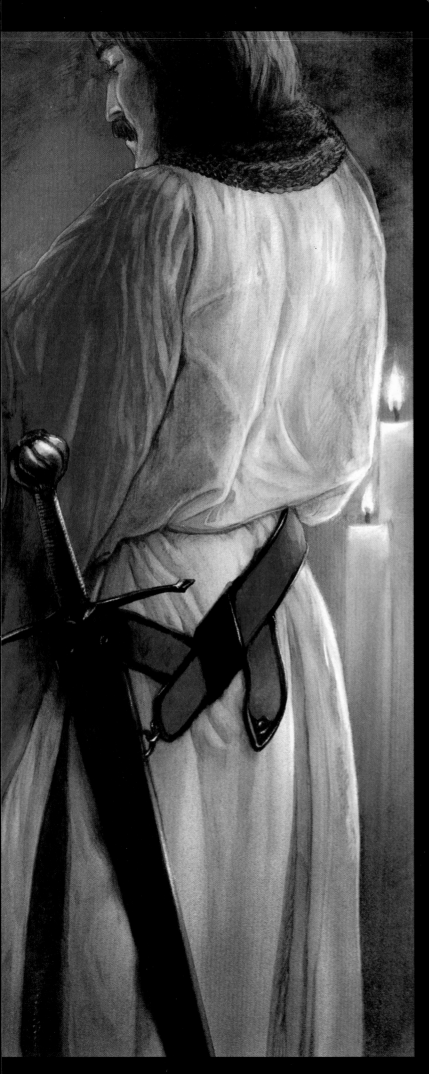

The Quest of the Fair Unknown

This is the tale of a man who sought to find his rightful place in the world by fighting the forces of enchantment. To prove himself, he ventured into lands that were strange to him and pitted himself against enemies who were more than human.

He was a man without a name. He rode one day into the hall at Caerleon of Arthur, High King of Britain, asking to enter the King's service. This young man could not tell the company who he was; he had been reared in a fortress in the mountains of the north. His mother, who ruled the territory without a husband, had seen that he was taught the arts of a courtier and the skills of war. His name she could not or would not tell him; nor would she say who his father was. When he reached the age of manhood, she sent him out into the world to seek his fortune.

King and company courteously heard the stranger out. Then Arthur nodded. It was clear that the golden-haired youth was gently bred, clear from his easy seat on his horse and his battered armor that he was a fighter.

"We will give you a name until you find your own. We call you Bel Inconnu—the Fair Unknown," said the King. Then he looked at his knights. "Who will stand for this young man?"

A man without a name came to King Arthur's court at Caerleon. So fine a man was he that he was given knighthood; he was called Bel Inconnu.

Gawain, weathered but still as golden-haired as the youth, stepped forward; Gawain was as generous to younger knights as he was merciless to enemies on the field. Lancelot joined him, so that the two finest men in Arthur's company served as sponsors for the stranger. They stood beside him for the ceremonial bathing and for the long night's contemplative vigil that preceded knighthood in those days. In the hour just at dawn, Lancelot gave the Fair Unknown a handsome broadsword; Gawain gave a gilded shield on which a crimson griffin ramped. So the Fair Unknown became the youngest in Arthur's band of warrior brothers, sworn to defend the King and all who sought the King's protection.

In those times, many petitioners came to the King. Arthur and his men had established peace in Britain, but in the wildernesses of the kingdom—remote territories where humans rarely ventured—masters of the old magics still held sway. Some were wonderfully seductive. Some were malevolent. All were dangerous, because they took men and women out of the safety of their own world into regions where mortals should not go.

The fledgling knight had therefore not long to wait for adventure; within days of his arrival, a young woman came into Arthur's hall to beg the court's aid. She was travel-stained and weary, but she bore herself proudly, and the tale she had to tell caused a stirring among Arthur's men.

The woman's name was Hélie; she was lady-in-waiting to the Queen of Wales, whose lands lay to the north of Caerleon,

The handmaiden of the Queen of Wales begged Arthur to aid her mistress.
This quest against enchantment became a test of valor for Bel Inconnu.

near the slopes of Snowdon. That Queen
was now in beast form, changed to a serpent through the sorcery of two brothers
who wanted her in the service of elder magic. Her prison was the echoing halls of her
own palace; her guards were dead men,
and all her lands lay waste. She had sent
Hélie away when she knew her own danger, and the young woman had ridden
south to Arthur, with only a dwarfish servant for company. Hélie asked now for a
knight to challenge the ancient enemies
and restore life to the land.

"Let my sword serve this lady," cried
Bel Inconnu, when Hélie's story was done.
The lady frowned, and the older knights
raised their brows: This was a task for a
proven champion. But Gawain strode to
the young man's side, smiling for his courage. Arthur raised his hand in token of assent, and the choice was made.

When Bel Inconnu joined Hélie in the
courtyard at Caerleon the next morning,
he found her cold and angry. He could
understand this: How was a nameless, un-
tried knight to aid her Queen? He greeted
her kindly despite her sullenness. She
wheeled her horse ahead of his and led him
away, and she made no effort to speak
above the clattering of the hoofs on the
courtyard paving stones.

Hélie grew more amiable, however, in
the days of riding that followed. They
soon left the fields and farms of Caerleon
and headed north, pursuing narrow tracks
through forest so vast and uncharted,
so crowded with bodiless voices and unknown beings that sages gave the place

*In the wild lands of Wales, Bel Inconnu battled a knight who guarded an
enchanted fortress. Its fairy mistress stole the young man's heart away*

no name but "Perilous." Bel Inconnu remained gravely courteous to the Queen of Wales's messenger, and he was alert in her defense, fighting the beings the forest sent against them—outlaw knights who lived by rape and robbery, even ancient giants, it was later said. Those he defeated he sent to Caerleon to give Arthur service, as was the custom then.

These forest skirmishes were no more than rehearsals for the tests that lay ahead. As the two neared Snowdon, the land grew high and rough. They finally cleared the woods on a chill November afternoon. At once, they halted. Before them, a river ran through a deep ravine. Near its opposite bank stood an islanded castle, bristling with black towers. A stone causeway bridged the water to the fortress, and this causeway was walled on either side with rows of blood-encrusted pikes, which pierced the shredded flesh of the necks of a score of helmeted heads—knights who had dared this place before. At its center, braced on widespread feet, was the sentinel of the causeway, a giant of a man, armored in mail with a surcoat of scarlet.

"Come and fight me, young one, if you are a man." The stranger's challenge howled through the cold air and echoed against the rock of the chasm's side.

"Come away," Hélie whispered, backing her palfrey toward the edge of the great wood. But no knight could refuse a challenge. Bel Inconnu dismounted and gave his reins into his companion's hand.

"Wait for me here, lady," he said. Unsheathing his sword, he strode toward the

Into the dead city of the enchanted Queen of Wales, the knight rode, and deathly palace guardians watched his progress through the silent streets.

causeway. He was met at its edge by the stranger, and within seconds the two men were locked in battle. In the dying light, they lunged and feinted and swayed on the bridge, grunting and cursing amid the clang of steel on steel. They fell apart, lurched toward each other again, and scythed the air with their great swords. At last, with a gurgling scream, one of them fell silent. It was the sentinel, and Bel Inconnu stood over his body, while at his back the fortress gate swung open, letting out a stream of golden light. In its arch was framed a garden, where trees flowered and birds sang, although the year was dying and in the Perilous Forest the leaves were dry and brown. A woman stood in this garden, tall and straight and pale, her hair an aureole of light around her head. She beckoned. Hélie rode forward then, leading the knight's horse.

"This is an enchanted palace," Hélie said. "That lady is no mortal woman; this is no place for a mortal knight." But Bel Inconnu obeyed the pale one's gestures. He crossed into the fortress, and Hélie had no choice but to follow with the horses.

They spent that night in the golden woman's garden. She fed them; with the lightest of touches, she healed the young knight's wounds; she said he had delivered her from the imprisoning sentinel; and she said that he must stay with her.

"He cannot stay," replied Hélie. "He has vowed before the King to save my lady of Wales." Her jaw was set; there was a militant sparkle in her eyes, and she was flushed with anger.

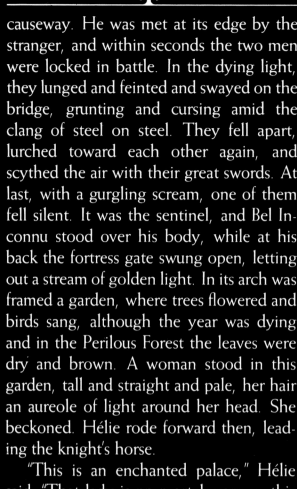

An adversary waited in the Queen of Wales's palace, an adversary who attacked Bel Inconnu with axes that flew at him as of their own will.

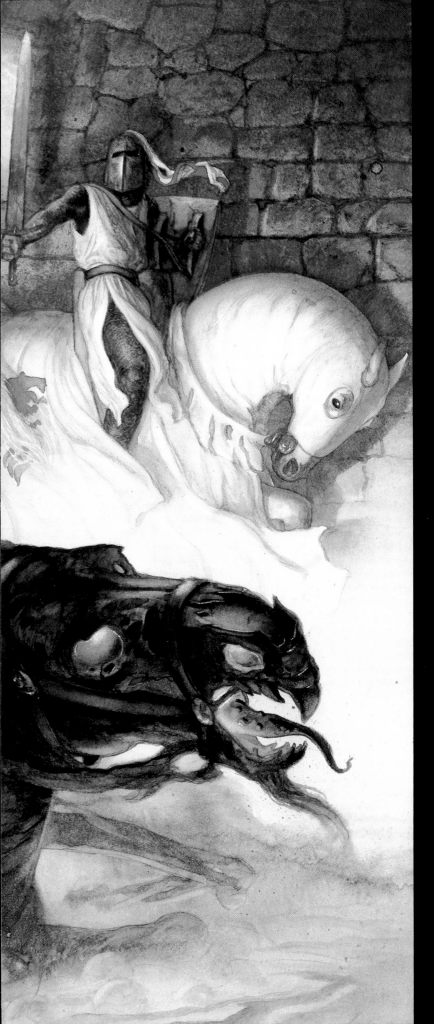

What she said was true. The young knight withdrew his gaze from the golden woman and straightened his shoulders. The fairy smiled at that and said, "Why, then, he will return, when his task is done. My world offers only pleasures."

And when morning came, the messenger and her knight pushed on into the windy mountains. They sheltered one night more, at the fortress of the man who was seneschal to the Queen of Wales and who guarded the borders of her territory. His was the last living land before the waste began. Here, Hélie, having led the knight to the verge of the Queen's city, rested. Her task was done: Bel Inconnu had then to fight alone.

And late one chill afternoon, the knight rode forth. On a track that wound up the bleak sides of Snowdon he rode, past bare trees nodding in the mountain wind, through rustling carpets of dead leaves, to a place where a high wall barred his way. Its blackened gate swung loose on its hinges; his horse shied, but at the knight's command, it moved forward through the gate.

An empty, cobbled street stretched before Bel Inconnu. Crumbling houses lined one side, huddled against the city wall, houses whose doors stood open and whose shutters banged in the wind. On the other side of the street, a vast palace stretched high and pale into the gloom of the gathering dusk.

A voice hailed him, and he looked up. Deep windows lined the palace wall above his head. In each embrasure, a torchbearer

The second assailant to confront the questing knight was a sorcerer whose horse breathed fire; sorcerer and horse melted at the mortal's sword stroke.

tood. These creatures wore black; the dim and flaring lights they bore revealed their skull-like faces and their empty, burning eyes. They sang of death and called the knight to join them. He cursed them and rode on until he found an archway that led into the palace hall.

There the enemy waited, standing huge and silent in the shadows. He had a man's shape, yet he was no man: Light from another world glittered in his darting eyes. The young knight's horse shook its bridle and stamped, but it held its ground. Drawing his sword, Bel Inconnu shouted the challenge. The sorcerer gave no answer, nor did he move. But a battle-ax, whistling in the air, sailed toward the young knight. Its edge bit the griffin on his shield. A second ax followed, and then a third and a fourth. They circled, hovered around the head of Bel Inconnu, slicing viciously toward his helmet, swooping upon his sword arm. Above them in the windows of the hall, the torchbearers now faced the interior, gazing down, grinning their death's-head grins.

His horse reared and screamed, and the knight charged the sorcerer. His sword met emptiness: The man had vanished into shadow. Released from command, the axes fell harmlessly to the paving stones of the hall.

Then the shadows gathered themselves into a shape, and an armored figure, mounted on a horse that spat gouts of fire, loomed over Bel Inconnu. He stabbed at the thing blindly; his sword sank into a mass of softness. A sick stench ex-

When he had vanquished two enemies, a third trial awaited Bel Inconnu: a glowing serpent that glided toward him and wrapped him in strong coils.

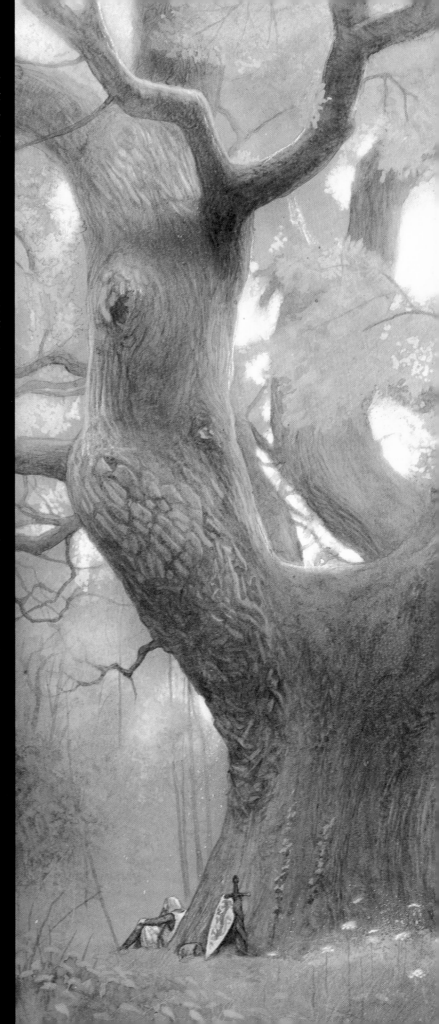

oloded in the air. The knight's assailant shrieked once. Then, before the young man's eyes, the shadow warrior and mount dwindled and sank to the floor, dissolving into a stinking, spreading pool of liquid. Horse and rider writhed in the corruption until at last the animal's fiery breath was quenched. At that instant, the torchbearers' lights went out.

Trembling with fatigue, Bel Inconnu waited in the pitch-darkness for the next attack. But there was no attack. Points of light appeared in the shadows, growing brighter as they approached. They were made by the jewel-like eyes of an enormous serpent that swayed toward him and, rising from the floor, enfolded him in its coils. Its eyes stared into his; its tongue flicked delicately toward his lips, and a voice sounded in his head.

"You are Gingalin, son of Gawain, hidden and nameless until you proved your worth and earned your name." Blackness pressed upon the young man's eyes then, and he fell, absorbed into the dark.

He awoke in sunlight, stiff and sore, but alive. He lay in the marble hall, whose high windows glittered with morning. Beside him a fair woman stood, regarding him thoughtfully.

"I am the Queen of Wales," she said, when she saw that he had awakened. "Mabon and Evrain clothed me in serpent's form so that they might have the kingdom for their kind. Your courage sent them from this world; your touch freed me. You will be Wales's King."

Gingalin stared at her. Then he rose

His trials over, his quest accomplished, the knight who now knew his name wakened alone in a forest. The time had come to take his rightful place.

and stumbled from the hall to the street outside, where his horse waited quietly. He himself had been touched by enchantment: His desire was not for the mortal Queen he had rescued but for the fairy woman, waiting in her gardens among her dark towers. He fled to her, as she had said he would, and knew no more of the Welsh Queen while he lived wrapped in a dream in a world that was not his own.

The fairy herself released him, however. The storytellers said that on a summer night when they walked under the stars, she bade him farewell and told him that mortals' power was stronger than her own now. Arthur summoned him, she said. He must go to Caerleon and join his fellows and the woman who would be his Queen and mother to his children. He could not stay in the fairy woman's world or he would fade from life altogether.

She said no more that night, but in the morning, Gingalin awakened not among the airy hangings of her bed, but on the ground in a clearing in a forest. His armor lay beside him; his horse cropped the grasses nearby. The black-towered castle was nowhere to be seen.

Then Gingalin took up his rightful life. He returned to Caerleon; he married the Welsh Queen, who awaited him there. In triumph he rode with her to her own lands and found them crowded with people and blooming with life, restored to health by his own valor. With his mortal Queen he ruled them all his life, and if he dreamed dreams of an other world where he might not go, he did not say.

Bel Inconnu – Gingalin, son of Gawain – took a wife and a kingdom at last. She was Wales's Queen, whom he had rescued from enchantment.

Acknowledgments

The editors wish to thank the following persons and institutions for their assistance in the preparation of this volume: Ancilla Antonini, Scala, Florence; François Avril, Curator, Département des Manuscrits, Bibliothèque Nationale, Paris; Otto Buhbe, Till Eulenspiegel Museum, Schöppenstedt, West Germany; Giancarlo Costa, Milan; Danmarks Paedagogiske Bibliotek, Copenhagen; Clark Evans, Rare Book and Special Collections Division, Library of Congress, Washington, D.C.; Marielise Göpel, Archiv für Kunst und Geschichte, West Berlin; Dieter Hennig, Brüder-Grimm-Museum, Kassel; Christine Hofmann, Bayerische Staatsgemäldesammlungen, Munich; Heidi Klein, Bildarchiv Preussischer Kulturbesitz, West Berlin; Roland Klemig, Bildarchiv Preussischer Kulturbesitz, West Berlin; Kunsthistorisches Institut der Universität, Bonn; Cecilia Östlund, Assistant Librarian, Svenska Barnboksinstitutet, Stockholm; Christine Poulson, London; Luisa Ricciarini, Milan; Dieter Scheller, Till Eulenspiegel Museum, Schöppenstedt, West Germany; Justin Schiller, New York City; Robert Shields, Rare Book and Special Collections Division, Library of Congress, Washington, D.C.; Siegfried Sichtermann, Kiel, West Germany; Mariann Tiblin, Scandinavian Bibliographer, University of Minnesota Libraries, Minneapolis; Lena Törnqvist, Librarian, Svenska Barnboksinstitutet, Stockholm.

Bibliography

Afanas'ev, Aleksandr, *Russian Fairy Tales*. Transl. by Norbert Guterman. New York: Pantheon Books, 1975.

Arnason, Jón, comp., *Icelandic Legends*. Transl. by George E. J. Powell and Eiríkur Magnússon. London: Richard Bentley, 1864.

Barber, Richard:
The Knight and Chivalry. New York: Harper & Row, 1982.*
The Reign of Chivalry. New York: St. Martin's Press, 1980.

Beaujeu, Renaut de, *Le Bel Inconnu* (Les Classiques Français du Moyen Age series). Ed. by G. Perrie Williams. Paris: Librairie de la Société des Anciens Textes Français, 1929.

Bettelheim, Bruno, *The Uses of Enchantment: The Meaning and Importance of Fairy Tales*. New York: Random House, 1977.*

Browne, Edward Granville, *A Year amongst the Persians: Impressions as to the Life, Character, & Thought of the People of Persia*. Cambridge, England: Cambridge University Press, 1927 (reprint of 1893 edition).

Campbell, J. F., comp. and transl., *Popular Tales of the West Highlands*. Vol. 2. Detroit: Singing Tree Press, 1969 (reprint of 1890 edition).

Campbell, John Gregorson, comp., *The Fians; or, Stories, Poems, & Traditions of Fionn and His Warrior Band* (Waifs and Strays of Celtic Tradition, Argyllshire series, No. 4). New York: AMS Press, 1973 (reprint of 1891 edition).*

Cavendish, Richard, *King Arthur & the Grail: The Arthurian Legends and Their Meaning*. New York: Taplinger Publishing, 1979.*

Chadwick, Hector Munro, *The Heroic Age* (Cambridge Archaeological and Ethnological series). Westport, Connecticut: Greenwood Press, 1974 (reprint of 1912 edition).

Cooper, J. C., *Fairy Tales: Allegories of the Inner Life*. Wellingborough, England: The Aquarian Press, 1983.

Darnton, Robert, *The Great Cat Massacre and Other Episodes in French Cultural History*. New York: Basic Books, 1984.*

Davidson, Hilda R. Ellis:
The Road to Hel: A Study of the Conception of the Dead in Old Norse Literature. Cambridge, England: The University Press, 1943.
Scandinavian Mythology (Library of the World's Myths and Legends series). London: Hamlyn, 1983.

Davis, Elizabeth Gould, *The First Sex*. Baltimore: Penguin Books, 1973.

Delarue, Paul, *The Borzoi Book of French Folk Tales*. Transl. by Austin Fife. New York: Alfred Knopf, 1956.

Donaldson, Bess Allen, *The Wild Rue: A Study of Muhammadan Magic and Folklore in Iran* (The Middle East Collection series). New York: Arno Press, 1973.

Duby, Georges, *The Knight, the Lady and the Priest: The Making of Modern Marriage in Medieval France*. Transl. by Barbara Bray. New York: Pantheon Books, 1983.

Foster, I. L., and Glyn Daniel, eds., *Prehistoric and Early Wales*. London: Routledge and Kegan Paul, 1965.

Fraser, George MacDonald, *The Steel Bonnets*. New York: Alfred A. Knopf, 1972.

Gallant, Roy A., *The Constellations: How They Came to Be*. New York: Four Winds Press, 1979.

Grafenberg, Wirnt von, *Wigalois: The Knight of Fortune's Wheel*. Transl. by J. W. Thomas. Lincoln, Nebraska: University of Nebraska Press, 1977.

Gregory, Lady, ed. and transl., *Gods and Fighting Men: The Story of the Tuatha De Danaan and of the Fianna of Ireland*. Gerrards Cross, England: Colin Smythe, 1979 (reprint of 1904 edition).*

Grimes, W. F., *The Prehistory of Wales*. Cardiff, Wales: The National Museum of Wales, 1951.

Grimm, Jacob, *Teutonic Mythology*. Vol. 1. Transl. by James Steven Stallybrass. Gloucester, Massachusetts: Peter Smith, 1976 (reprint of 1883 edition).

Grimm, Jacob Ludwig Karl, and Wilhelm Karl Grimm:
The Complete Grimm's Fairy Tales. Transl. by Margaret Hunt. New York: Pantheon Books, 1972.
Sixty Fairy Tales of the Brothers Grimm. Transl. by Alice Lucas. New York: Weathervane Books, 1979.

Grønbech, Vilhelm, *The Culture of the Teutons*. Vols. 1 and 2. Transl. by W. Worster. London: Oxford University Press, 1932.

Hamilton, Edith, *Mythology*. New York: New American Library, 1969 (reprint of 1940 edition).

Harvey, Paul, *The Oxford Companion to English Literature*. Oxford, England: Oxford University Press, 1981.

Harward, Vernon J., Jr., *The Dwarfs of Arthurian Romance and Celtic Tradition*. Leiden, Netherlands: E. J. Brill, 1958.

Heller, Julek, *Knights*. New York: Schocken Books, 1982.

Hole, Christina, *English Folk-Heroes*. London: B. T. Batsford, 1948.

Hugon, Cécile, *Social France in the XVII Century*. New York: The Macmillan Company, 1911.

Jacobs, Joseph, *More Celtic Fairy Tales*. New York: Dover Publications, 1968 (reprint of 1894 edition).

Jenkins, J. Geraint, *Life & Tradition in Rural Wales*. London: J. M. Dent & Sons, 1976.

Jobes, Gertrude, *Dictionary of Mythology, Folklore and Symbols*. New York: The Scarecrow Press, 1962.

John, Brian, and Inger John, *Scenery of Dyfed*. Lanchester, England: Greencroft Books, 1976.

Jones, Gwyn, and Thomas Jones, transls., *The Mabinogion*. London: J. M. Dent & Sons, 1976.*

Karr, Phyllis Ann, *The King Arthur Companion*. Privately published, 1983.

Keen, Maurice, *Chivalry*. New Haven, Connecticut: Yale University Press, 1984.

Kellett, E. E., *The Northern Saga*. London: Leonard and Virginia Woolf, Hogarth Press, 1929.

Keyser, R., *The Private Life of the Old Northmen*. Transl. by M. R. Barnard. London: Chapman and Hall, 1868.

Leach, Maria, ed., *Funk & Wagnalls Standard Dictionary of Folklore, Mythology and Legend*. 2 vols. New York: Funk & Wagnalls, 1949.*

Loomis, Roger Sherman:
Studies in Medieval Literature: A Memorial Collection of Essays. New York: Burt Franklin, 1970.
Wales and the Arthurian Legend. Cardiff, Wales: University of Wales Press, 1956.

Lungbergh, Holger, transl., *Great Swedish Fairy Tales*. New York: Seymour Lawrence, 1973.

MacCulloch, J. A., *The Childhood of Fiction: A Study of Folk Tales and Primitive Thought*. London: John Murray, 1905.*

MacManus, Seumas, *The Story of the Irish Race: A Popular History of Ireland*. Old Greenwich, Connecticut: Devin-Adair, 1983 (revision of 1921 edition.).

Mandrou, Robert, *Introduction to Modern France, 1500-1640: An Essay in Historical Psychology*. Transl. by R. E. Hallmark. London: Edward Arnold, 1975.

Manguel, Alberto, and Gianni Guadalupi, *The Dictionary of Imaginary Places*. New York: Macmillan, 1980.

Massignon, Geneviève, *Folktales of France*. Transl. by Jacqueline Hyland. Chicago: The University of Chicago Press, 1968.

Moncrieff, A. R. Hope, *Romance of Chivalry*. North Hollywood, California: Newcastle Publishing, 1976.

Nielsen, Kay, *East of the Sun and West of the Moon: Old Tales from the North*. Garden City, New York: Doubleday, 1977.

Ólason, Vésteinn, *The Traditional Ballads of Iceland: Historical Studies*. Reykjavik: Stofnun Árna Magnússonar á Íslandi, 1982.

Olrik, Axel:
The Heroic Legends of Denmark. Transl. by Lee M. Hollander. New York: The American-Scandinavian Foundation, 1919.
Viking Civilization. Rev. by Hans Ellekilde. New York: The American-Scandinavian Foundation and W. W. Norton, 1930.

Olrik, Axel, comp., *A Book of Danish Ballads*. Transl. by E. M. Smith-Dampier. Freeport, New York: Books for Libraries Press, 1968.

Opie, Iona, and Peter Opie, *The Classic Fairy Tales*. New York: Oxford University Press, 1974.

Pálsson, Hermann, and Paul Edwards, *Legendary Fiction in Medieval Iceland*. Reykjavik: University of Iceland, 1970.

Payne, Robert, *Journey to Persia*. New York: E. P. Dutton, 1952.

Phillips, Roger, *Wild Flowers of Britain*. London: Pan Books, 1977.

Plath, Iona, *The Decorative Arts of Sweden*. New York: Dover Publications, 1966.

Pyle, Howard, *The Story of King Arthur and His Knights*. New York: Marathon Press, 1978.

Ranke, Kurt, ed., *Folktales of Germany*. Transl. by Lotte Bauman. Chicago: The University of Chicago Press, 1966.

Reader's Digest Association, *Folklore, Myths and Legends of Britain*. London: The Reader's Digest Association, 1973.

Rooth, Anna Birgitta, *The Cinderella Cycle*. Lund, Sweden: C.W.K. Gleerup, 1951.

Ross, Anne, *Pagan Celtic Britain: Studies in Iconography and Tradition*. London: Routledge and Kegan Paul, 1967.

Rowling, Marjorie, *Life in Medieval Times*. New York: G. P. Putnam's Sons, 1968.

Saxo Grammaticus, *The History of the Danes*. Vols. 1 and 2. Ed. by Hilda R. Ellis Davidson, transl. by Peter Fisher. Cambridge, England: D. S. Brewer, 1979 and 1980.

Schach, Paul, transl., *Eyrbyggja Saga*. Lincoln, Nebraska: The University of Nebraska Press and The American-Scandinavian Foundation, 1959.

Schofield, William Henry, *Studies and Notes in Philology and Literature*. Vol. 4. Boston: Ginn & Co., 1895.

Shah, Idries, *World Tales*. New York: Harcourt Brace Jovanovich, 1979.

Sommer, H. Oskar, ed., *The Vulgate Version of the Arthurian Romances*. Vol. 2. *Lestoire de Merlin*. New York: AMS Press, 1969 (reprint of 1908 edition).

Southwold, Stephen, *The Book of Animal Tales*. New York: Thomas Crowell, 1935.

Sutcliff, Rosemary, *The High Deeds of Finn Mac Cool*. New York: E. P. Dutton, 1967.

Thompson, Stith:
Motif-Index of Folk Literature. 5 vols. Bloomington, Indiana: Indiana University Press, 1955.
One Hundred Favorite Folktales. Bloomington, Indiana: Indiana University Press, 1968.

Tongue, Ruth L., comp., *Forgotten Folk-tales of the English Counties*. London: Routledge & Kegan Paul, 1970.

Tremain, Ruthven, *The Animals' Who's Who*. London: Routledge & Kegan Paul, 1983.

Vaughan-Thomas, Wynford, *Wales*. London: Michael Joseph, 1983.

Vicary, J. Fulford, *Saga Time*. London: Kegan Paul, Trench, 1887.

Ward, Donald, ed. and transl., *The German Legends of the Brothers Grimm*. Philadelphia: Institute for the Study of Human Issues, 1982.

Weston, Jessie L., *The Legend of Sir Gawain: Studies upon Its Original Scope and Significance*. New York: AMS Press, 1972 (reprint of 1897 edition).

Wilber, Donald N., *Iran: Past and Present*. Princeton, New Jersey: Princeton University Press, 1948.

* Titles marked with an asterisk were especially helpful in the preparation of this volume.

Picture Credits

Correspondents: Elisabeth Kraemer-Singh
(Bonn); Margot Hapgood, Dorothy Bacon
(London); Miriam Hsia (New York); Maria
Vincenza Aloisi, Josephine du Brusle (Paris);
Ann Natanson (Rome). Valuable assistance
was also provided by: Ardis Grosjean,
Gevene Hertz (Copenhagen); Millicent
Trowbridge (London); Felix Rosenthal
(Moscow); Mary Johnson (Stockholm).

Chief Series Consultant

Tristram Potter Coffin, Professor of
English at the University of Pennsylva-
nia, is a leading authority on folklore.
He is the author or editor of numerous
books and more than one hundred arti-
cles. His best-known works are *The British Traditional Ballad in North America, The
Old Ball Game, The Book of Christmas Folklore* and *The Female Hero.*

This volume is one of a series that is based
on myths, legends and folk tales.

Other Publications:

UNDERSTANDING COMPUTERS
YOUR HOME
THE KODAK LIBRARY OF CREATIVE PHOTOGRAPHY
GREAT MEALS IN MINUTES
THE CIVIL WAR
PLANET EARTH
COLLECTOR'S LIBRARY OF THE CIVIL WAR
THE EPIC OF FLIGHT
THE GOOD COOK
THE SEAFARERS
WORLD WAR II
HOME REPAIR AND IMPROVEMENT
THE OLD WEST

For information on and a full description
of any of the Time-Life Books series listed
above, please write:
Reader Information
Time-Life Books
541 North Fairbanks Court
Chicago, Illinois 60611

Library of Congress Cataloguing in
Publication Data
Main entry under title:
Seekers and saviors.
   (The Enchanted world)
   Bibliography: p.
   1. Tales.   2. Fairy tales.
I. Time-Life Books.   II. Series.
GR76.S43 1986   398.2   85-24587
ISBN 0-8094-5249-9
ISBN 0-8094-5250-2 (lib. bdg.)

Time-Life Books Inc. offers a wide range of
fine recordings, including a *Big Bands* series.
For subscription information, call 1-800-621-
7026 or write TIME-LIFE MUSIC, Time &
Life Building, Chicago, Illinois 60611.